The
CRYSTAL
POOL

The CRYSTAL POOL

MYTHS AND LEGENDS OF THE WORLD

GERALDINE McCAUGHREAN

Illustrated by
Bee Willey

Margaret K. McElderry Books

By the same author and illustrator

The Golden Hoard:
Myths and Legends of the World

The Silver Treasure:
Myths and Legends of the World

The Bronze Cauldron:
Myths and Legends of the World

For Ailsa
If I could I would give you all the stories in the world
G. M.

For Lucette A.
Without whom nothing would have been possible
B. W.

Margaret K. McElderry Books
An imprint of Simon & Schuster Children's Publishing Division
1230 Avenue of the Americas
New York, NY 10020

First published in London by Orion Children's Books
First United States Edition, 1999

Book design by Dalia Hartman
The text of this book is set in Garland Light.
The illustrations were rendered in mixed media.

Printed in Italy
10 9 8 7 6 5 4 3 2 1

Library of Congress Catalog Card Number: 98-85103
ISBN: 0-689-82266-9

Contents

Four Worlds and a Broken Stone

A NATIVE AMERICAN MYTH

THE PEOPLE of Peace will tell you that three worlds existed before this one, and before that a Nothingness flowing from never to ever.

Taiowa, though invisible himself and without form, pictured a solid universe. So he created a creator — Sotuknang — to be its architect. Sotuknang shaped the First World, called Endless Space, and into it, down a thread as fine as one of his own hairs, dropped Spider Woman, fat with the eggs of magic. Those eggs hatched into the very first people.

If you met them, of course, you would hardly recognize them as kin. There is not much of a family resemblance. For they, those most ancient of our ancestors, never grew old, never spoke, and never hunted the animals with whom they shared Endless Space. Also, they had no tops to their heads. Taiowa was able to drop wisdom into their minds like golden

1

honey off a spoon. No learning by their mistakes, no puzzling or studying, no struggling with the meaning of things. Understanding came to them as sweetly as honey, and in among it were the seeds of language.

After a while, the People of Endless Space were muttering to one another, passing comment on the world around them. The animals, alarmed by this new secret, tried to speak themselves. But beaks and muzzles and snouts are not made for more than calling a mate, warning of danger. Noticing the difference between them, the animals drew away, hid among the trees and down burrows, thinking, "They are ganging up against us."

Far from it. The People of Endless Space no sooner had language than they began to quarrel — to lie, to boast, to curse and shout insults. Some drew away from the rest, hoarding their treasure of words like money they begrudged spending.

Sotuknang was disgusted. Like a blacksmith who throws bad work back on to the forge, he lit a fire under that world called Endless Space, and burned it to the ground.

The people saw the flicker of fire, and there was sweet wisdom enough in their heads for them to observe the animals, and learn from them. When they saw the ants run underground, the people followed, sheltering deep under the earth from the inferno. When they emerged, a Second World had been built: a world called Dark Midnight. It was gloomy and a little scary. At either end — at North Pole and South — sat giant brothers, steadying the globular world.

Living underground had forced shut the people's open-topped heads somewhat, so now they found it harder to understand what the gods wanted them to do. Still, one or two things they did invent that Sotuknang had never even thought of. For example, instead of sharing everything, they *sold* what they had for money, or exchanged it for goods. "What do you mean, you can't afford it?" they would say. "Nothing comes for free in this life!" They began to haggle, to cheat one another, to steal what they could not afford. Soon the streets of the world were full of people crying their wares.

They sold food to the animals and sold the animals to each other. They sold the land they stood on and the water in the rivers. In the world called Dark Midnight, they sold candles to one another, and complained that times had been better once, in the world of Endless Space.

"Enough!" said Sotuknang. "Twin of the North! Twin of the South! Leave your places! The mind of God requires *Change!*"

Twice the earth rolled over as the Twins let go of its axletree. The round world was as shaken as a pebble in the surf. Oceans slopped over the dry land. Cargo ships far out to sea were picked up and dashed down on marketplaces miles inland. The deserts drowned, and with them the scaly salamanders and crackling locusts. Freshwater rivers were lost in a saltwater surge, and with them the herons and the turtles.

But the people — some of them at least — had the wit to follow the ants belowground again. And the sea had no sooner withdrawn than out they crawled to inspect the Third World left by the tidal waves: Kuskuara.

Ideal building land. They shaped adobe, they made mud bricks, they cut stone blocks and cut down timber. They built cities in wood and stone and brick and clay, with houses and temples, meeting halls and silos. Before long, someone said:

"Our city is better than your city."

"Our land stretches to the horizon!"

Banners declared: "Trespassers will be stoned. Keep out."

Generals proclaimed: "We must fight for what we believe in!"

The people answered: "WAR!"

From the bones of trees and the feathers of birds, they built flying machines, and swooped over rival cities showering them with rocks and pitch. Their enemies built newer flying machines to do combat in midair with the bomber flying machines, and when flying machines crashed onto the crowded cities, ran with buckets to put out the fires.

At last there were so many fires that only Sotuknang could put them out. His tears swelled the oceans until the oceans joined hands and bled one into another. Whole cities, whole city-realms drowned — even the ants beneath them. Whole continents softened into mud and slid away, and with them the shape and existence of Kuskuara.

But the people — some of them at least — had had the wit to climb into hollow reeds and float away on the rising water. Bobbing about over acres of ocean, the survivors of Kuskuara kept a lookout for land. But there was no land left. Seagulls perched on the reeds and, riding out the flood alongside them, flew in search of dry land. But they came winging back, beaks outstretched, sagging wearily into the wave troughs, exhausted for want of solid ground to rest on.

"Peace, peace," said Spider Woman. "I who saw Endless Space and Dark Midnight, who saw Kuskuara come and Kuskuara go, shall live to see more worlds yet. For if the mind of Taiowa wishes a world to exist, then he won't rest till he has succeeded."

She was right, of course. One morning they looked out across the oceans and saw land. The Fourth World had come into being: World Complete.

Standing on the shore was a gigantic man — huge, terrifying, his eyes alight with visions he was seeing in his head, and in his hands a hammer and chisel such as sculptors use to carve rock.

"Come ashore!" he told them. "I am Masaw, Guardian of the World Complete. Come ashore! I have things to tell you."

Masaw had dreamed dreams. Though the top of his head was closed, the gods had found surer ways of imparting wisdom to this wise giant. He took them inland to a place called Four Corners — a desert landscape planted with towers of dark rock. On one such mesa, Masaw had carved the story of his dreams. The people threw down their bundles of belongings and began to scrape together the dirt for building homesteads.

"No!" said Masaw. "Not yet! You are not yet fit to settle in the Complete World! You have truths to learn, wonders to see, problems to solve." Picking up a large, flat stone, he broke it, as easily as a biscuit, into four equal parts. Then he parted the people into four groups according to the color of their skin — red, yellow, white, and black — and gave each group

one fragment of the stone. To North, South, East and West he sent them, far and wide over the face of the Complete World. "Come back when you have done journeying and meanwhile remember just one thing."

"What must we remember?" asked everyone, eager to obey.

"Never to forget," replied Masaw.

First to come home were the red tribe. Long before the continental plates bumped and groaned into their present positions, the red tribe were back, building their villages around the Black Mesa, calling themselves the Hopi, which means "Peace." They read Masaw's carvings now and trembled: his dream carvings spoke of unspeakable terrors to come. But what, and why?

When the white tribe came back, they had forgotten everything — their piece of stone, the words of Masaw, their narrow escape from fire and flood. They did not recognize the red tribe as their brothers — nor the yellow, nor the black. In fact, they came home armed with guns and swords and firebrands, ready to fight or kill or capture anyone who stood in their way. They peered at the Black Mesa with eyes as blind as drunkards, seeing only a jumble of words and pictures, understanding nothing.

"See here?" said the Hopi gently. "This bowl of ashes falling out of the sky? It will scorch the dry land and set the oceans boiling!"

But the white tribe could only see scribbles and scrawls.

Now, luckily, it is your turn. Look closer. See that blue star drawn on the Black Mesa? One night, when the Fourth World has burned down, wick and wax, and left only a puff of smoke behind, the time will have come for a Fifth World, a final world, just as Taiowa intended, just as Sokutnang wished, just as Masaw dreamed, just as the People of Peace long for. See that blue star? Watch for it. Everything else has happened just as Masaw said it would. So watch out for the blue star rising.

Lamia

AN INDIAN LEGEND

HE THOUGHT that he came on the place by chance, but that was not quite true. A deer led him to it. Ali Mardan Khan followed the creature deep into the forest, to the shores of a lake, before it eluded him among green shadows. Not two moments later, he heard weeping.

A woman sat with her back to a tree, her hair braided with wires of gold and silver, her dress bright with mirror sequins, so that she glistened like a fallen star. At the sight of him, she stretched herself at his feet, hands clasped in supplication.

"Don't be afraid," said Ali Mardan, raising her up. "You're on my land here, and no harm will come to you. But who are you?"

She said she was a princess from over the mountains — from war-torn China. "My father was defeated in battle. Of all my family only I escaped.

8

I have wandered for weeks through the mountains." Not one jet-black hair was out of place, not a fold of her dress creased, but he believed her instantly. For surely the gods had reached out to preserve this unearthly beauty. The flower boats that plied his Kashmiri lakes were no lovelier than Princess Amali, her voice so soft, sibilant, and sweet.

"You are welcome to make my home your own," said Ali Mardan.

"If you were to offer me marriage, I would not refuse," said the Princess, looking shyly through her lashes. His fate was sealed.

There on the banks of the lake, Ali Mardan built his bride a palace in keeping with her loveliness. She wanted peace and solitude, she said, and to be alone with him; he was only too glad to agree. Only one thing marred those beautiful early days of marriage: Ali Mardan began to suffer fearful stomach pains.

"Let me nurse you," said Amali. "I'm gentler than those brutal physicians of yours with their leeches and scalpels." And so tenderly did she care for him, night and day, that Ali Mardan every dawn reproached himself for feeling no better.

One day, as his manservant helped him walk about in the garden, breathing the scents of the forest, they came across a wandering holy man, small and bony as a pigeon, asleep under a tree.

"Shall I throw him out of your garden, sir?" asked the servant.

"Certainly not. Holy men are a blessing from heaven. Fetch a bed out here, and have food prepared for him when he wakes. I must lie down now. The pain, it's too . . ."

When the holy man woke, he was delighted to find himself on a soft couch surrounded by trays of food. He sought out his host to thank him. "I am sorry to find you unwell, sir. Perhaps I can repay your kindness with my own humble knowledge of medicine."

He examined Ali Mardan, asked questions, and strummed his lower lip, rapt in thought. "Are you by any chance newly married, sir?"

"Why, yes! I am!"

The man smiled. "Then the remedy is plain, and I shall supply it! Let me cook dinner tonight."

He picked all the herbs, ground all the spices. But although he cooked exactly the same meal for Ali Mardan as for the Princess, he sprinkled a handful of salt over Amali's plate. If she noticed, she said nothing and the meal passed without incident.

By midnight Amali had a raging thirst. She got out of bed, and went to the water jug. But the jug was empty. She went to the door. But it was locked. She went to the window. But its grille of wrought iron was designed to keep out thieves: no way out.

With a glance at her sleeping husband, Amali stretched herself, reaching up as though she would touch the ceiling. Her body grew thinner; her bones seemed to melt away. Her skin glistened green in the moonlight, and her hair congealed to her back and legs. A serpent ten feet long reared up from the patch of moonlight where Amali had stood a moment before, its jaws agape for water, forked tongue flickering. Out between the filigree ironwork of the window she slithered, and down to the lake, drinking her fill, dislocating her serpent jaws to scoop up the water. Then she slithered back to the palace.

In the shadow of the wall stood the holy man, a little silver hatchet in his hand. The moment her head was through the bars, he struck. But the snake was too quick for him, the scales too tough.

Next morning Ali Mardan summoned the holy man to his room.

"I'm sorry, sir. I wounded her, but I could not kill her."

"Wounded whom? Is there an assassin loose in my palace?"

"No, sir. A lamia."

If for two hundred years a snake lives unseen by human eyes, it becomes a dragon. A hundred years more, and it becomes a lamia — a creature of infinite wickedness, able to change into any shape — a bird, a tiger. Worse, it can become a woman and feed on the lifeblood of a man.

"Your wife, sir," said the holy man, "is poisoning you with the venom of her kisses. Your only cure is to kill her."

"Never! No! You're wrong! Aha, I can prove you're wrong! You may have wounded some snake in my garden last night, but not Amali. I left her asleep in bed. Unhurt! See for yourself: here she comes!"

But as Princess Amali entered the garden, her silken cloak blew back:

they saw that one of her arms was in a sling. "I dropped my mirror. I cut myself," she said when she saw them staring.

When she had gone, Ali Mardan drew a trembling breath. One hand clutched the pain in his side, one gripped the arm of his chair. "Tell me what I must do," he said at last, "to kill a lamia."

They built a summerhouse of shiny lacquered tree bark, down by the lake. It had just a table, a chair, a bed, and a big oven.

"Come with me, Amali," said Ali Mardan. "The holy man thinks one of my courtiers may be poisoning me. So I shall eat nothing but what is cooked by your own hand, and have no one near me but you."

The Princess looked doubtful. "Cook, my love? But I hardly know how . . . being a princess, you know. Besides, I hate ovens."

"Only a loaf of bread," he said. "You can hardly refuse me that."

The walls of the summerhouse were so thin and fine that the shadows of husband and wife could be seen as they kneaded dough together at the table. The smaller shadow turned to place the bread in the oven. The taller moved painfully across behind — and gave her a push.

Into the oven went the lamia! And Ali Mardan staggered from the hut, his arm across his face. Servants came running with blazing torches, and set light to the summerhouse: it burned like a chrysanthemum bursting into crimson bloom.

Next day, Ali Mardan woke feeling stronger. He dimly hoped the pictures in his head were left over from some bad dream. But when he climbed out of bed and found his body free from pain, he realized that the death of the lamia — his bride — had truly taken place.

Outside the door stood the holy man, traveling-staff in hand. "I can safely leave you now, sir, and return to my monastery. But come with me to the lake, if you will."

"Must I?"

The summerhouse was nothing but a pile of ash around the cast-iron oven. Opening the oven door the holy man swept out a handful of ash and a pretty green pebble. "Choose: the pebble or the ash?"

"The pebble," said Ali Mardan without thinking.

"Then I shall keep the ash," said the holy man.

Ali Mardan sat the pebble down on the oven while he stared out across the lake. The lilies were just coming into bloom. Birds were eating seed from the rushes, dragonflies hovering over their reflections. When he turned back, the oven was solid gold.

He pocketed the stone with a smile. "And what can the ash do?" he asked. But no one answered. The holy man had disappeared among the trees, and Ali Mardan would never know what the ash of a lamia could do. He was glad it had gone. He used the alchemy of the pebble only rarely, when he most had need. It reminded him of his dead wife and the gleam of gold wire in her braided hair.

A Question of Arithmagic

A LEGEND FROM ICELAND

IF ALL the villains in the world were stupid, it would not matter whether or not kings were wise. But many of the wickedest people are dangerously clever, and most cunning of all are the trolls.

Fortunately, Olaf Tryggvason was not merely a king, he was a scholar, too. He could read, write, and add up; sometimes even do all three at once. The warriors who manned the oars of his ship were strong and fearless, loyal and handsome — men like Thorgeir the Bold — but they held the King in awe and admiration because he was a scholar and a thinking man.

Sailing one day through the dank Icelandic mists of winter, King Olaf commanded his navigator to steer close by the cliffs. "If we keep land within sight," he said, "we cannot lose our way in this infernal fog." So carefully, gingerly, the dragon-prowed ship moved along the rocky coastline, close enough inshore to see gannets and cormorants riding on the updraft, close enough to see seals sleeping in the coves, sea pinks growing in the rocky crevices. They sailed so close, they even caught sight of an old man balanced precariously on a narrow shelf of rock halfway up the cliffs. The King hailed him through cupped hands.

"Are you stranded?" he called. "Do you need help?"

"Not at all," the old man called back in a voice clear and strong. "Greetings, King Olaf Tryggvason. Hail and all hail." Something about the voice made Thorgeir miss his oar-stroke.

"What's your name? Where do you live?" called the King, for it was a wild, inhospitable coast with not a house in sight.

"I live in this cliff, of course: I and all my fighting men."

King Olaf was intrigued. He knew nothing of any warlord living in this part of his kingdom, nor of any army, although he made it his business to know such things. "And how many men do you command, sir?"

The old man began to chant:

> "Twelve ships have I with oaken keels;
> In every boat there ride twelve crew.
> Each rower kills a dozen seals,
> To make our daily meal of stew,
> And cuts each skin in twelve and then
> Each strip is cut in twelve again;
> Each portion cut must serve ten men:
> How many are my followers, then?"

The King laughed and clapped his hands. A riddle! There was nothing he liked better. Calling for paper, he began to work the problem out. "Twelve ships and each one has twelve . . . that's one hundred and forty-four rowers . . ." The King sucked the feather of his pen and frowned as he struggled with the mathematics.

Thorgeir, meantime, noticed a certain sideslipping motion of the ship. The birds of the cliff seemed bigger than before.

"One hundred and forty-four rowers kill twelve seals each: that's . . . one seven two eight . . ." The King's quill scratched busily.

Thorgeir, meantime, stood up to get a proper look at the old man on the cliff. He seemed to be chanting under his breath. More poetry, perhaps? Or then again, perhaps not.

"One thousand, seven hundred and twenty-eight sealskins, all cut into twelve," mused the King. "That's four, carry one — eight — one, carry one . . . By the gods, this man has a bigger army than I do . . . !"

Thorgeir, meantime, felt a faint grating on the ship's hull. It was being pulled steadily inshore, closer and closer to the snarling rocks. As a whirlpool sucks ships into its swilly mouth, the old man's chanting was dragging the King's ship to its destruction. "Your Majesty . . ." he began.

"Don't interrupt, I'm multiplying," muttered King Olaf, and went on counting imaginary strips of sealskin.

The old man was clearly visible now, much closer than before. Thorgeir could see how his yellow eyes glinted and his snaggled teeth were bared

in an evil grin. The oarsman pulled his oar out of the rowlock, but it was too short for the job. He cut through the sheets of the mainsail and heaved the mast itself out of its socket in the deck. Resting it on the ship's rail, he put his chest against its end and prepared for a jarring shock.

"... and if each portion feeds ten men ..." muttered the King.

"I think, master, that this old man ..." grunted Thorgeir, struggling with the weight of the mast.

"You'll make me lose my place," said the King, bending over his sums.

Then the tip of the mast struck the cliff with a force that broke three of Thorgeir's ribs. Still, he strained to hold the ship away from the cliff that would rip out its side.

The old man on the cliff, seeing Thorgeir's efforts, scowled at him and chanted faster and louder, a magic chant, a troll chant to wreck the King of Iceland. He cursed Thorgeir, with all the black arts of trolldom.

The magic dragged on the ship as though the very cliff were a magnet and the ship a twopenny plug of iron. Thorgeir felt his breastbone bend, his heart falter within him, but still he held the ship off the cliff.

"So I make that fifty-one thousand, eight-hundred and ..." said King Olaf Tryggvason. But his answer was never finished. With a noise like a lightning-strike, the mast snapped as, with one final mighty effort, Thorgeir levered the dragon-prowed ship out into deeper water. That great jerking thrust was enough to break the power of the old man's magic. He had to watch his prize escape him, pitching and rolling out of harm's way.

The King lost his footing and fell on his back, ink spilling over the workings of his sum. Looking up, he was in time to see the old man on the cliff change back into his rightful shape — three coils of a hideous nose, and a face like moldy cheese. "By the gods, it was a troll!" he cried. "D'you see that, Thorgeir? It was a troll trying to lure us onto the rocks!"

Thorgeir said nothing, but lay in the bottom of the boat, content to have saved the King and his comrades from a miserable death on the rocks. "It is a wonderful thing," he consoled himself, "to have a scholar for a king."

But a bit of common sense doesn't go amiss, either.

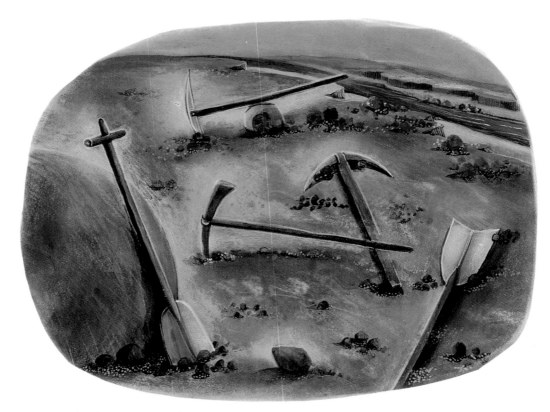

The Gods Down Tools

A SUMERIAN MYTH

"ENOUGH!" SAID Enki, throwing down his spade. "For a thousand years we've dug out rivers and piled up hills. There has to be more to life than this!"

Around him, the other gods nodded and muttered. Spade after pickax dropped to the ground. "Let Enlil do it himself!"

It was a surly rabble of weary immortals that picketed the home of Enlil, Lord of the Winds. "What's the matter?" Enlil asked when he came to the door. "Why have you stopped working? You still have the River Tigris to dig! We must have that bend in the river by Monday!"

"We're sick of digging," said the gods. "You've worn us out, Enlil. We're all agreed: no more digging."

To their astonishment, Enlil burst into tears. "I'm sorry! I never realized. I was a fool! I resign as world-planner! I do, I resign!"

The strikers shuffled their feet, embarrassed and a little shamefaced. The Lord of the Winds was a sensitive, passionate soul; they had not meant to hurt his feelings.

We-e coughed awkwardly. "Suppose — just suppose," he said, "that we created some kind of creature to do the work for us?"

And thus humankind was invented — Nintur made them out of earth and blood — to finish digging the river and planting the fields.

They did very well, worked as industriously as the ants, *and* worshiped the gods as well, which gave the gods a warm and happy feeling they had not felt before. Nintur did not need to make thousands: they reproduced themselves. And when they were worn out and could not work anymore, they died. Cities grew up, like anthills, with homes and shops, bathhouses and meeting halls. Carts trundled from place to place, and street sellers shouted all day long:

"Buy your fish! Fresh fish today!"

"Lots of lovely lemons!"

"Cage-birds, songbirds, going cheap!"

"W H AT I S T H AT D I N ?" demanded Enlil one day.

"It's the People," Enki replied. "Busy little things, aren't they?"

Enlil groaned and covered his ears. "The noise! The racket!"

Now Enki had grown rather fond of humankind, and the noise did not much trouble him — except perhaps women who sang off-key and crying babies at night. "Each separate one doesn't make much noise. It's just that there are so many these days."

"Then *thin them out!*" hissed Enlil, his nerves frayed from lack of sleep. "Send Plague to kill them, one in three."

Regretfully, Enki summoned Plague and told her. But then he hurried ahead to the cities of Sumer, and warned the workers.

When Plague arrived, everywhere was silent. The cartwheels were muffled with cloth, the babies were all feeding, women passed by their neighbors without a word, and street sellers mimed on the street corners. What is more, delicious offerings were burning on every altar. Plague had not the heart to slaughter one in three, not even one in ten. Not one, in fact.

Enlil did not insist. The cities were silent. He was able to sleep at night and snooze in the afternoon. And he needed workers to build the Zagros Mountains.

For a thousand years, all went as well as it can in the best of all possible worlds. Parents told their children to be quiet, but the children forgot to tell their children. The noise gradually increased. Husbands nagged their wives, children squabbled over toys, women insisted on singing, in and out of key.

"Where can a god go to have some peace and quiet, with this chatter-chatter-chatter?" Enlil complained. "Let the rivers dry up, let the lakes turn to salt. Perhaps when they are dead of thirst, these human beings will be silent!"

Enki hurried down to the cities of Sumer and warned them: unless they quietened their noise, a fearful drought would kill whole families, neighbor-hoods, towns! The priests rushed to the temples of An, the water god, and heaped them with gifts. The men held their fingers to their lips, babies sucked their thumbs, and the din once more fell silent. An had not the heart to take their water, and Enlil had gone back to sleep.

For a thousand years all went as well as it can in the best of all possible worlds. Parents told their children to be quiet, and their children told theirs. But then someone said the story of the drought had never hap-pened. A woman argued with him, and people took sides. Tempers flared, punches were thrown, and the fight that followed made more noise than all the street-traders in Sumer.

Enlil closed his windows. Enlil closed his doors. But still he could hear the din of the cities of Sumer. "I WILL NOT HAVE THIS NOISE!" he bellowed. "If they must open their mouths to shout and jabber, let them have no food to put in them, and let them starve and die, but GIVE ME SOME PEACE!"

The famine began instantly; there was no time for Enki to warn anybody. Crops withered, trees cankered, the berries were eaten by birds. The People grew thin as sticks, and had nothing but water to give their children. They called on Enki to save them.

But how to help? Enki paced the banks of the Tigris, stalked the fruitless woods, thinking. Then with a cry of inspiration, he ran to the

river and threw in a handful of magic.

Thirty thousand fish tumbled down the river — a coppery shoal of bream and carp overspilling the banks and leaping clear of the waves. There were so many that the People had only to reach out a hand to grasp a fin, a tail, a fishy feast. After that, their mouths were too crammed to talk. Also, fishing is a quiet pursuit, so that Enlil, though angry, let the famine end. "Next time . . . ," he muttered. "Next time . . ."

For a thousand years, all went as well as it can in the best of all possible worlds. Parents told their children to hush, and their children told their grandchildren. But babies will cry, and neighbors will quarrel. A man must sell his wares. People laugh at jokes, and children cry when they fall over.

Enlil tried to sleep on one ear, then he tried to sleep on the other. But the noise of the cities of Sumer was howling pandemonium in his head.

"AWAY WITH THE LOT OF THEM!" he thundered. "Let the earth know silence again. Drown every mortal!"

With the winds in his keeping, he piled up the waves of the sea and thrust rain into the rivers till they burst their banks. He plugged up the tunnels under the earth and gathered the rain clouds like a flock of sheep. This time Enki could see no way to save the People: no possible way . . . unless he were to save just one. . . .

"Beware! Beware, Atrahasis!" he whispered to the best of his mortal friends. "The Lord of the Winds is sending a flood! Build a boat — a big boat — and take your family aboard, along with two of every kind of animal. . . ."

Perhaps you have heard this story, or some version of it.

For seven days and seven nights water rolled down the rivers and cascaded out of the sky, drowning all the crying and laughing, shouting and music, traffic and building and singing. The last sounds to trouble Enlil came from swimmers crying for help to the gods, and rooks shrieking in the drowning trees. Then everything was silent.

The gods looked down in horror at the world they had dug and shaped and peopled. They saw their altars and the flowers from their altars float by on the Flood. All this for the sake of peace and quiet?

As the Flood soaked away, Atrahasis' boat ran aground on a mountaintop,

and he set loose the animals. They plowed, muddy-legged, through the ruined crops and fallen buildings, the wreckage of the Flood.

"We must offer thanks to the gods that we were saved," was the first thing Atrahasis said.

When Enlil woke from his peaceful sleep, he looked down at the empty earth and saw . . . Atrahasis.

"Kill him!" he cried, bursting into tears. "Kill him, or he'll breed! I can see it now! People marrying, people multiplying! Soon it will be as bad as ever! Kill Atrahasis!"

He gave the order, but none of the other gods moved.

"Kill him!" screamed Enlil, making more noise than anyone.

"I'm hungry," said Enki.

"The fields need tending," said Nanna. "Who will do it, if not Atrahasis and the sons and daughters of Atrahasis?"

"There's a lot of *mending* to be done," said An pointedly.

"Must we do it all ourselves?" said We-e.

"Must we do everything?" they asked. And one by one, Enki led the gods away, leaving Enlil amid the silence of solitude.

They say Atrahasis was a soft-spoken man, and that he raised his children to speak softly, too. Even with all the gods but one on his side, Atrahasis knew better than to take chances.

A Bouquet of Flowers

AN ABORIGINAL MYTH

IT WAS from a piece of the sun that Baiame made the world, but his home was among the stars, and it was there that he returned when his work of creation was done.

"Don't cry, little ones," he told the people and animals as he said good-bye. "I have to go. Otherwise you would forever run to me with your troubles — like children never learning to grow up. You know I love you and that I'll still be watching over you from my home." He pointed to the galaxy of the Milky Way stretched like a silver hammock across the night sky.

The animals nodded their heads and wandered off, far and wide. The men and women also understood, but stayed waving long after Baiame the Creator had risen into the sky. Some lay down on soft clumps of flowers to gaze up at the sky and remember their long talks with the Father Spirit. Then they, too, got up and walked home, thoughtful, wistful, trailing tardy feet through the flowers that carpeted every fold and furrow of the shining new earth. Wherever Baiame had trodden, flowers had sprung up: every color of the rainbow and a thousand shades between — scarlet, umber, purple, gold and white. From horizon to horizon they cloaked the rocky ground, cushioned and pillowed it into the sweetest of resting places.

But what were those flowers feeling now? Flowers have no power of reason, no instinct to guide them. They could not comprehend why dear Baiame, who had given them life, should no longer be nearby.

So some migrated. Like birds in winter, they rose in huge flocks, fledged with their own petals, flying, flying toward the object of their love. Into the sky they fluttered, on outward into space, swagging the sky with coronas of color. The rest died.

Soon the air was filled with cries of women searching, searching, then realizing that there was not a single flower left living on the whole bare, brown face of the earth. The air was filled with something else, too — with swarms of frantic bees searching in noisy millions for one speck of pollen, one sip of nectar. There was no golden honey to be had, either, and life was much less sweet in those drab days after the flowers died.

In time, of course, the sadness faded. Those who remembered the flowers grew old. Naturally, they told their grandchildren about them and the wonder that had once been, but the grandchildren hardly believed such far-fetched fairy tales. Those children, as they grew older, remembered talk of flowers, but not, of course their colors. Who can remember something they have never seen, or describe it to their grandchildren? So flowers bloomed only in the mouths of storytellers — a wonder of times long gone. And color was only in the skins of animals, in insects and the sky, in fishes and the sea. And in the eyes of the storytellers.

Watching with gentle multicolored eyes, Baiame felt sad at this one flaw in the earth's loveliness. So one night, along with the starlight, he rained down dreams on sleeping humanity. Those with listening hearts were stirred by a voice. They seemed to hear it telling them to make a journey. By first light they set off — like sleepwalkers unable to resist the yearning within them. And every man, woman, and child who answered the yearning found that their journey brought them to the selfsame spot. From north and south, near and far, hither and yon they came, to the mountain where Baiame had long ago stepped off into space — and to which he had now returned!

There he sat, reaching out his arms like a father inviting his children to sit on his knee. "Come with me, little ones," he said. "I have something to give you."

Gathering them up into his hands, into his hair, into the crook of his arm and the folds of his robe, he carried them into the sky and on out into space, to where the Milky Way stretched like a silver hammock. He took them over dunes of darkness to valleys invisible from Earth . . . and their cries of amazement set the stars swinging.

For there lay swathes of color they had never seen before, colors even their women of vision had not dreamed nor their painters imagined.

"These are the 'flowers' you storytellers speak of," said Baiame. "Pick them. Pick as many as you can carry, and take them back with you to the earth. On the day I took a piece of sun and made the world for you, I meant there to be flowers. You have been without them too long. So take them, and when they die, sprinkle their seed on the brown ground, and I will send warmth and rain enough to make them come again."

In sheaves and armfuls they reaped flowers and carried them down out of the sky. Like conquering heroes they returned to their separate villages, laden with color, to astound their families and amaze their friends with bouquets of such dazzling glory that it seemed a rainbow had crashed to Earth and scattered its debris over their homes.

And though Baiame's helpers were not able to carry as many flowers as had once bloomed on Earth, they took enough to paint every corner of the world with every color in the mind of God.

The Pied Piper

A GERMAN LEGEND

ONE DAY Frau Fogel put her hand into the bread box, and something brushed against it, warm and furry, that sank its teeth into her palm and drew blood.

Next door, Frau Reuzel went to kiss her baby, and found something gray and sleek curled up against the baby's cheek, the cot full of droppings.

At the inn, the innkeeper opened his cellar doors and was met by a flood of fur, a sea of rats that washed over his feet and streamed away into every corner, squealing.

The little town of Hamelin was infested with rats. Not a house was free of them, not a corner safe to set down a child or a plate of food. Rats moved along the Mayor's white tablecloth, even while the Mayor ate his dinner. Evil, filthy, beady-eyed, with tails like earthworms and teeth like needles, they no longer ran away from the brooms that tried to sweep them out-of-doors, but chewed on the broom bristles and swarmed where they pleased.

"Get rid of them! Please!" pleaded the people, banging on the Mayor's door. "Do something, or what do we pay taxes for?"

"I sent the public rat-catcher, didn't I? With his bucket and pole," said the Mayor from an upstairs window. "What more do you want?"

"But the rats ate him!"

"And his bucket!"

"And his pole!"

"Do something!"

It was at this moment that a stranger arrived in town. He attracted stares, but no friendly greeting, for he was an odd-looking creature in multicolored clothes like a jester — one stocking green, one red, one sleeve blue, one yellow. He wore his hair long, slicked down against his head and shoulders, and a jacket with long tapering tails right down to his dusty boots. He played a pipe, too, and Hamelin was not accustomed to music; the people there had never yet discovered what purpose it served, what profit was to be made from it.

The children liked him, of course, but then children are notoriously bad judges of character. They like a person because he makes them laugh, and ignore a man with ten thousand in the bank. In the town square, the stranger raised his pointed nose in the air and cocked his head, as if those small, round ears so high up on his head could hear something out of the ordinary.

"What d'you want?" shouted the town beadle. "Keep right on going. We have rodents enough round here already."

"Perhaps I can help you, then. . . ." said the stranger.

He said that he could rid the town of rats. For one hundred gold pieces, he would drown them in the river and end the plague.

"Give him the money! Give it!" shouted the crowd gathered outside the Mayor's house. "Pay the Piper!"

"Anyone can make grand promises," said the Mayor. "But can he keep them? First let him do it, and then I'll pay!" From the eaves and sills, crouched on shop signs and along the rim of the ornamental fountain, a million rats looked on with glittering eyes.

"A hundred pieces of gold when I've rid you of rats," said the stranger. And the Mayor blustered, "Yes, yes."

So the Piper put his pipe to his lips and played a tune. It had four beats to the bar, because rats go on four feet. It had a bleak, gray, scampering squeal that set everyone's teeth on edge. But the rats loved it.

The rats were spellbound by it. Captivated. Out of the houses and drains, the gutters and lofts and cellars, out of the cradles and cupboards, the bread boxes and rubbish, the water butts and covered carts, a tide of gray vermin swirled down toward the playing of the pipe. Men and women alike screamed at the sheer number — they had never realized! — old men fainted at the stench. But the Piper just went on playing, strolling down toward the bridge, toward the river.

He sank them in the river: he played them to their deaths. Rafts of rats floated down the Weser River, their tails trailing like so many extinguished candlewicks. A strange silence replaced the ceaseless whistle of rodents squealing, the ceaseless scrabble of their claws. There was only the pleasant sound of children playing. Nothing but the rats' droppings and their teethmarks in the cheese remained to prove they had ever been there. And those were soon cleared away.

"What rats!" said the Mayor when the Piper asked for his money. "I see no rats. I recall no rats."

"You promised me one hundred gold pieces."

"Promised? I remember no promise."

The Piper turned toward the stallholders in the marketplace. He was wearing black and white now — pied like the thieving magpie — though no one had seen him change his clothes, or could see where he had carried such baggage. They heard his argument with the Mayor, but they said nothing. After all, the hundred gold pieces would have been paid out of *their* taxes.

"Pay him!" said a child. But then children have no sense of business. They would squander money on anything.

Then the Pied Piper put his pipe to his lips and played another tune. For a man cheated out of money it was a remarkably cheerful tune — a dance, a caper full of laughing trills. And it had *two* beats to the bar.

The children loved it. The children were captivated by it. Enchanted. Throughout Hamelin they left their desks, their toys, their books and games. The older ones picked up their baby brothers and sisters and carried them. They walked and skipped and danced and toddled down toward the bridge and over the river.

Their parents were busy — so much to do now that the rats had gone. They did not realize what was happening. A strange silence replaced the crying of babies, the chant of children playing or reciting their lessons. It was not until the schoolmaster stood at his school gate, screaming himself blue, that the parents noticed their children — all their children — topping a rise on the mountain road, following the Pied Piper. Following, following. Leaving, leaving, leaving them behind.

How those mothers and fathers ran and called and hallooed. Shoes sliding in the dirt, aprons clenched in fists, shouting children's names, shouting

promises: "We'll pay you! A hundred golden pieces! A *thousand* gold pieces! *Come back!*"

The Koppenberg Hill resounded with their shouts, shook with them. It fractured and tore itself apart, opening a rift in the rocks as great as a cathedral door. In at the door went the Pied Piper and behind him the children, without a backward glance. The hill healed itself, closed and knit so completely that no trace remained of the door by the time mothers started clawing at it with their bare hands. *"Don't go! Come back!"*

The human heart does not mend so easily as rock, and that day every heart in Hamelin was broken.

"It's your fault they're gone! You should have paid him!" they shouted, beating on the Mayor's door. "Where are our children!"

"Children? What children?" said the Mayor in terror. "You have no children now. Forget them! They're gone. What purpose did they serve, in any case? What are they good for — babies, children? I never understood. Work! Profit! They're the only things that really matter! That's all we have to worry ourselves about now. Work! Profit! And —"

"Death!" cried the people of Hamelin as they stormed the Mayor's house like a pack of ravenous rats.

A Prickly Situation

A NATIVE AMERICAN MYTH

BEAVER HAD been beavering away all summer. Busy, busy, busy. His dam was built, he had plenty of food for the winter. "My larder is full," he said, congratulating himself as he pushed an arrowhead ripple across the pool with his nose. "Not like hers," he thought as he saw Porcupine sitting idly on the bank. She was still sitting there later in the day. "*My* larder is full," Beaver thought gleefully as he pushed another ripple back across the pool, swimming homeward.

His larder was empty.

Beaver caught up with Porcupine on a forest path, pushing a large wheelbarrow full of food. "You stole my food, you bone-idle bunch of no-good knitting needles!"

"Me? Never. I'm a porcupine. Porcupines don't steal," replied Porcupine.

Beaver took a look into the wheelbarrow. The food was familiar. Beaver-type food. So he went to take a large bite out of Porcupine's nose.

At the last moment, Porcupine tucked in her nose and fanned out her spines. It was like biting on a pincushion. Beaver jumped backward, yelping and whimpering, with a noseful of spines, while Porcupine rattled away, swinging her rump about like a mace.

When the Beaver People saw the state of Beaver's nose, they felt the hurt as though it were their own. "This is war!" they declared. "That porcupine has eaten her last dinner!"

An army as huge and plush as a bearskin laid siege to Porcupine's house, and when she would not come out, knocked it down and dragged her away. This time they used ropes. There wasn't a thing Porcupine could do to save herself. Over leaves and stones, over beach and out to sea they towed the thief, marooning her on an island seven miles offshore. Not husband, child, friend, or neighbor could find hide or spine of her, though they searched and searched.

Dismayed and discomforted, Porcupine listened to the rhythmic splash of her enemies' oars as they rowed away and left her. Then shaking herself, with a noise like spillikins, she looked around the island. No berry bushes, no farm crops, no shops. There was not even so much as a tree to chew the bark off, not a string of seaweed washed up on the beach. "They mean me to starve!" said Porcupine, choking back a sob. "Well, I shan't give them the satisfaction! I'll drown myself in the sea! . . . in a minute or two." Being an idle creature, Porcupine sat down for a rest.

A gentle breeze was blowing across the island, and in it the first bitter seeds of winter. Also a voice. At least, it *sounded* like a voice in Porcupine's ear, saying, *"Call the North Wind, your kin! Call on the North Wind!"*

Porcupine was not of a mystical turn of mind. She had no faith in chants or spells. So she paid no heed — only hunched and slumped her way around and around her barren prison until, in her hunger, she could count her ribs as easily as her spines. Her eyesight was smeary and her ears rang. They rang with that same voice: *"Summon the North Wind, your kin! Summon up the Wind!"*

Porcupine had nothing to lose, and there was no one close by to snigger, so she lifted up her nose and sang the chant:

"Come you North Wind, full of winter!
Come you North Wind, full of snow!
Come you steel-gray, glass-sharp splinter
in the sky's eye, North Wind BLOW!"

Spiny with hail and sleet, rattling and bristling with icicles, the North Wind heard, and came howling down from the Arctic. There were no trees to groan or bend, no beasts but Porcupine to shiver in the icy blast. But the sand swirled in eddies across the beach, and the sea slopped gelatinous against the shore.

Yes, the sea gelled and stood still. Its waves were trapped under a crust of ice as, gradually, the sea froze solid as far as the horizon. Sadly, poor Porcupine was too feeble to move, too weakened by hunger to crawl out on to that magic ice and escape!

Porcupine's relations, searching the shoreline, were amazed at the sight of the sea freezing over. They set off at once across its furrowing, fretful surface, to search all the islands offshore. Last of all, they came to a knoll so small and bare, they would never even have spotted it but for the dark spiny shape rolled up in a ball on the sand. Porcupine!

She had to be carried home and fed cabbage broth through a quill straw. The sight of her was so piteous that her family quite forgot the crime that had been her undoing. "This is war!" they declared. "That beaver must pay!"

An army as prickly and numberless as the conker shells under a chestnut tree stormed Beaver's lodge. And though his huge dam proved as impenetrable as a castle wall, the porcupines did manage to take one prisoner. Beaver himself was captured and dragged away, over mud, over stones, and through the forest.

"You marooned Porcupine and left her to starve! Now we'll maroon you, Rug-tail!" They dragged him over tree roots and up the trunk of a tree. Like a lynch mob they swung him from one branch up to the next, until he burst headfirst out of the very crown of the tree. "Bet you didn't know porcupines could climb trees, did you? Eh? Eh, Bugs-beaver? Now see how you like a taste of your own medicine!" And so saying they left him, abandoned him at the top of the tallest tree in the forest.

Around him a sea of trees waved in late autumnal tides of orange and gold. Beaver shook the leaves out of his fur and listened to the rattle of a dozen porcupines shinnying down the tree. Then he hummed a small tune to himself — not a magical chant or a mystical incantation — just a tune.

As he hummed, he began to gnaw. Gnaw, gnaw, gnaw. Beaver liked to keep busy. Busy, busy, busy. By next morning, he had gnawed his way through the entire tree, top to bottom. Then he trotted home to his pool, his dam, and his lodge under the dam, and spent a day or two gathering fresh supplies of food, then a peaceful winter relaxing with his family.

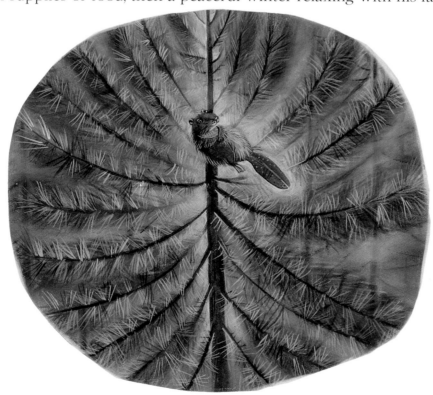

Race to the Top

A MAORI MYTH

IN THE very Highest Heaven, Papa Io prepared three presents for the Human Race. He took three baskets and into one put Peace and Love. Into the second he put Songs and Spells. Into the third he put Help and Understanding. The people of Earth would need all these if they were to get along with one another successfully. And Papa Io knew all about the importance of getting along. He had two sons, Tane and Whiro, who could no more agree than fire and water. He had put Tane in charge of light, Whiro in charge of darkness. The jobs suited their temperaments perfectly, he thought. For Tane was all brightness, kindness, and goodness, while Whiro (although Io wept to admit it) was gloomy, evil, and dangerous.

Naturally, when the three baskets were ready, it was easy to choose which son should deliver them. Io stuck his head out over Heaven's parapet and called through his speaking trumpet, "Tane! Come up here! I need you to take these gifts to Humankind!"

Now Whiro knew full well that whoever delivered such fine presents to the people of Earth would win them, heart and mind. They would never stop thanking or praising the messenger. The thought of praise appealed to Whiro. So, while Tane climbed the Great Tower of Overworlds, story by story, up the ladders that led from one floor to the next, Whiro set off to climb the *outside* of the Tower. Like ivy, like a fat black spider creeping silently up a wall, he raced his brother skyward, determined to reach the top first. In his pockets were all the tools of his trade, all the tricks that would give him the advantage. . . .

It was slow going. But by the time he reached the second story, Whiro found Tane was already on the third. So, out of his pocket he pulled handfuls of mosquitoes, sand flies, and bats. "Kiss my brother for me, my dearios," he said, and flung them in the air.

Unsteadily balanced on the ladder between worlds, Tane was suddenly engulfed in a cloud of flying black particles. They flew in his eyes, his ears, his mouth, and up his nose. He bent his head down against the swarm, clinging to the ladder with one hand while, with the other, he fumbled in his pocket. At last he tugged out a twist of North Wind as big as a towel, and waved it around his head. The insects and bats were swept by a frosty gusting gale miles out to sea.

So, when Whiro, climbing the outside of the Tower, reached the third story, Tane was already well on his way to the fourth. Whiro put his hand in his other pocket and drew out, like a fisherman's maggots, a handful of ants, centipedes, hornets, spiders, and scorpions. "Say hello to my brother from me, sweetlings," he said, and threw them in the air.

Halfway up the next tall ladder, Tane heard a crackling, and was suddenly, vilely beset by creepy-crawlies. They swarmed through his hair, infested his clothing; they stung his bare arms and cheeks and calves. Feeling in his pocket, he found no rags of wind, nothing at all to swat them away. There was nothing he could do but shut tight his eyes and mouth and go on climbing — higher and higher — from the eighth to the

ninth to the tenth story.

Gradually, the air became thinner, purer. The holiness emanating from the magic realms above filled the upper storys with a glorious perfume. The disgusting crawling creatures began to fall away, overcome, like mountaineers succumbing to altitude sickness.

Outside, on the wall of the Great Tower of Overworlds, even Whiro began to flag. His arms and legs ached. His fingers could barely grip. When he looked down, his head swam at the dizzying drop. He would never make it as far as the eleventh story before Tane.

Spotting a small window in the side of the Tower, Whiro slipped through it, feetfirst, and found himself on the ninth floor. Very well. If he could not catch Tane on the way up, he would ambush him on the way down. Hiding himself in the shadows behind the ladder, he settled down to wait. . . .

In the uppermost Overworld, welcoming hands helped Tane from the ladder and led him before Papa Io. And there, while pink evening clouds drifted between the white pillars of Highest Heaven, Io entrusted his three precious presents into Tane's keeping. "Give them to Humankind with my love and blessing," said Io. "And tell them to watch out for that infernal brother of yours. He's a tricky one, that Whiro, though I weep to say it about my own son."

Carefully, carefully, Tane started back down, the baskets balanced neatly on top of one another. The perfumes of Highest Heaven were heady, and he was feeling a little light-headed as he stepped onto the ladder from tenth to ninth Overworld. He had only one hand free to grasp the rungs now, and he could not properly see where to place his feet.

Suddenly a hand grabbed his ankle and wrenched him off the ladder. He fell, the baskets tumbling on top of him, on top of Whiro, who was just then sinking his teeth deep into Tane's thigh.

There in the darkness they fought, good and evil, sparks and foulness spilling from the folds of their clothing. Their panting breaths sped the clouds across the evening sky. Against a blood-red sunset, the Tower of Overworlds trembled and rocked, while the birds screamed around its shaken frame: "Help! Murder! Ambush!"

Whiro was rested. He liked a fight, liked to inflict pain, whereas his brother was naturally a gentle soul. But Tane knew, as his brother's hands closed around his throat to throttle him, that if Whiro once got hold of the baskets, he would either spill them or use them to take control of Earth and its people. He slapped feebly at his brother's chest, but there was no pushing him away. He reached out a hand across the creaking floor; his fingers brushed a fallen basket; the lid came off and rolled away into the darkness. A wordless song and a single magic spell spilled into Tane's open palm.

Suddenly a sacred, magic warmth crept up his wrist and arm, into his aching muscles, inspiring him to one last effort. Pushing Whiro backward, Tane toppled him over the edge of the hatchway and — *thud* — down into Overworld Eight; *crash* — down into Overworld Seven; *bang* — down into Six . . . and Five and Four and so, by painful stages, all the way down to the stony Earth.

He was not killed: immortals don't die. And the whole episode did not serve to sweeten his nasty temper. Picking himself up, Whirro snarled, "Not deliver the baskets? Well, then, I shall make Humankind some presents of my own! Sickness for one! Crime for another! DEATH for a third!" And he slouched away to find baskets big enough for all the miseries he had in store.

Tane delivered the three baskets safely to the people of Earth. So after that, they were armed against anything Whiro could hurl at them. The only lasting damage was to the Tower. Shaken and rocked by the titanic struggle on the ninth floor, its rickety structure teeters now, condemned, on the world's edge. It would not carry the weight of the smallest child, let alone the great bulk of Papa Io climbing down from the sky. So Humankind are on their own now. They will have to make do as best they can with what the gods gave them.

The Alchemist

A CHINESE LEGEND

MR. CHIA was a laundryman. All day he beat the soapy washing clean on a huge block of stone using a long wooden bat: a tedious, wearisome job. But he passed the time thinking about money and what he would do with it if he ever had any.

One day he saw a cart unloading furniture at a house nearby. Chia went at once to call on his new neighbor — his new and *wealthy*-looking neighbor — to introduce himself. But the gentleman seemed always to be out. In the end, Chia resorted to hiding in a bush and jumping out as the man put his key in the door. Then he bowed politely and presented a bottle of wine: "A gift of welcome from your humble neighbor," he said.

"Charmed, charmed," said the gentleman. "Come indoors and let us share this wine! My name is Chên."

It was a hot day. The wine slipped down deliciously, and the two got on well. There seemed nothing exceptional about Mr. Chên except perhaps his good looks and musical speaking voice. When the wine was almost gone, he fetched a large jade jug and poured the last drop into it.

At once the jug filled to the brim with the best wine Chia had ever tasted. "What a trick!" he gasped. "Can you do any more?"

Chên smiled benignly and took out a small shiny black stone. He spoke a few words, rubbed the stone against a vase — and at once the vase turned to silver.

Chia gasped. "Where did you get that stone? What is it? I want one! Where can I get one? Where?"

Mr. Chên sighed. "I was afraid of this. I was told in Heaven that you are a greedy man, Mr. Chia."

"Greedy? Me?"

"That's why I tried to avoid meeting you. You must understand: we Immortals are not permitted to teach alchemy to you mortals. Imagine the chaos it could cause here on Earth."

"Oh, absolutely. Chaos! I quite understand!" said Chia. "Have another drink."

Twenty drinks later, as Chên slithered like a pickled eel out of his armchair and onto the floor, Chia searched his robe, found the lodestone, let himself out, and went home.

It was no use, of course. He did not know the magic words, and so, although he rubbed pots, bottles, cups, melons, and the dog, his alchemy simply did not work.

It was some hours before Mr. Chên woke up. When he realized his lodestone was missing, he assumed he had lost it by sheer carelessness, and scoured the house, the garden, the street — even went over to the laundry to tell his neighbor of the disaster.

But Chia greeted him with good news as he opened the door: "Ah! My friend! I found something of yours this morning!"

"My lodestone?"

"Your lodestone, yes! In the street! You must have dropped it."

Mr. Chên was overjoyed. "How can I ever thank you! I should be in such trouble in Heaven if they found out I'd lost it!"

Chia bowed. "Don't mention it . . . only I suppose you might see fit to reward me by letting me use the stone. Just once!"

Chên was flustered. "Impossible! I mustn't! It's forbidden!" But Chia looked so hurt, made Chên feel so ungrateful and mean, that finally he agreed. "I'll show you — but you must *promise* not to be greedy. Change a few lead coins perhaps, or a pebble. Otherwise the gods are bound to find out what I've done."

"Something like this, say?" said Chia, holding up a small bar of soap.

Chên mopped his brow with relief. "Clearly the rumors I heard about you in Heaven were quite ill-founded!"

Chia put the tiny morsel of soap on the huge wash-slab where every day he beat the washing clean.

"Now say:

"As Earth is to Heaven, as little is to much,
Lodestone raise the nature of whate'er you touch."

Chia's fingers, clutching the shiny black stone, hovered for a moment over the sliver of soap as he spoke the magic words. . . . Then they dodged aside and quickly rubbed the wash-block. Instantly, half a ton of silver stood gleaming amid the laundry.

"No! *No!* What have you done?" cried Chên. "My name will be struck from the Book of Angels for this! How could you! What will become of me? No! No!" He rushed out of the laundry tearing his hair and reproaching Chia bitterly for his deceitful trick. But Chia hardly heard. He was busy staring at his reflection in the shining silver slab.

A year went by. One day, an elegant gentleman arrived in town and knocked at the laundry door, asking for Chia. But Mr. Chia was out: "At the hospital, probably," the gentleman was told.

He was on his way there when he met Chia coming the other way. The two recognized each other at once.

"My dear Chia!"

"My dear Chên! How have you been, all this time?"

"Not bad! Of course, at first my name was struck from the Book of Angels, as I said it would be. The gods were furious with me for sharing the secret of alchemy. But after you built the new school and all those houses for the poor, and the hospital, the monastery — those orphanages, and planted all those blossom trees . . . well, I was summoned to Heaven. 'We misjudged you, Mr. Chên!' they said. 'Through this man, you have done more good on Earth than we have managed in many a year. . . .' I must admit, though: for a time *I* misjudged *you*, my dear Chia."

"What? You didn't really think I'd spend all that silver on myself? With so much poverty all around me? I used to dream, while I beat those clothes, how I'd wash away a thousand miseries if I ever had the money. And you, my friend, you gave me the opportunity."

So they shared a bottle of wine, and parted. "Until we meet again in Heaven!" said Mr. Chên.

"You really think there's place in Heaven for a poor laundryman like me?" exclaimed Mr. Chia delightedly. "Ah well, yes, I suppose the angels need their clothes washed just like everyone else. Till we meet, then, in Heaven's laundry!"

Mommy's Baby

AN INUIT MYTH

EVERYONE KNOWS that babies are a treasure. But most have forgotten that once babies, like treasure, had to come by digging. All sons and daughters lay underground, like spring bulbs: girls near the surface, boys deeper down. And a woman who wanted a family had only to take a spade and go mining. Consequently, strong, fit, hardworking women had whole armies of children, whereas lazy women might have only one or two.

Then there were the accursed women — luckless wives who, dig as they might, never found the treasure they were seeking. Kakuarshuk was just such a woman. More than sleep, more than food, more than sealskin coats or a fine house, Kakuarshuk wanted a baby. But wherever she sank her spade, however deep she dug and for however long, she turned up nothing but ice and snow, lichen and frozen earth. Sometimes it seemed as if she had dug up all Greenland in her search.

In desperation, she went to visit an *angekkok*, a conjuror, who plucked magic out of the air rather than children out of the earth. "Please tell me!" cried Kakuarshuk. "Where must I dig to find a child? I've worn out five spades digging, and all I have to show for it is a basketful of loneliness!"

The *angekkok* scratched in the dirt with a magic stick — a map with glaciers and mountains and villages. "Dig here," he said, closing his eyes and driving the stick hard into the ground. "Here or nowhere."

The place was a great journey from Kakuarshuk's village, but she took nothing with her — only a spade over her shoulder and a great yearning in her heart. Like a gold miner she struck her claim. Like a prospector after diamonds she broke open the hard crust of the earth. No girl baby lay near the surface. But perhaps a boy lay deeper down, waiting for her, with joy clenched in his tiny fists. So Kakuarshuk dug and went on digging. Deeper than any reasonable woman would have dug, deeper than any woman had *ever* dug, Kakuarshuk shoveled up the soil, until the sky was no more than a gray speck high above her head. Through permafrost and fossil layers, rocky strata and soft loam she dug until, like a black mole, she was lost inside the very earth. When her spade broke, she dug on with the shaft until, exhausted, she lay down and waited to die.

A moment later, a spade sliced past her head, and sunlight streamed into her face. Somebody was tunneling in the opposite direction!

"Oh, yes! Yes! I have found one!" cried a voice. "A dear little lady one! Oh! Oh! My very own little mommy!"

A baby, huge as a polar bear, as pink and bare as a crayfish and without a tooth in her head, scooped up Kakuarshuk and hugged her close. Overhead, a brilliant blue sky spilled hot sunshine upon a green wonderland of flowers and trees. There was no ice, no snow in this land peopled with giant babies. Crawling, toddling, laughing, or crying, there were babies everywhere. Some were digging with little trowels, and some had already found what they were after. Here, on the other side of the world, the babies dug for mommies and, having found them, cradled them in their

arms, while the mommies grew younger (and wiser) day by day.

It took some getting used to for Kakuarshuk. She was accustomed to working hard all day, and yet here all she had to do was ride in the crook of her baby's arm and be sung to. The babies did everything for their mommies, fetching them food, washing and dressing them, settling them to sleep under the shade of the flickering trees.

Kakuarshuk explained, as she was dandled on her baby's knee, about her long journey through the earth, about the differences between her world and this. She told of her longing for a baby of her own. Her baby looked at her with tear-filled eyes.

"When you are young enough, my darling, I shall show you where to dig for your heart's desire. But you will need all your strength, so close those pretty eyes and go to sleep now. There's my good little mommy."

Kakuarshuk's child was true to her word. One day she took Kakuarshuk to a place called Troll Mountain, and gave her a scarlet trowel. "Dig here, my pet lamb," said Baby, "and never give up, come trouble, come terror, come troll. If you are spared, you may see your world again, though I'm sorry to lose you — sorrier than you will ever know."

Kakuarshuk began to dig. She dug so deep that soon the brink of the hole was no more than a speck of blue high above her. This time she struck a tunnel, and wandered along it, in utter darkness, hoping to find an exit on her own side of the earth. But the tunnel linked with others — with a maze of tunnels — and every one *dug by a troll!*

They pounced on her out of the darkness, huge grotesque beasts as white as slugs, with snuffling noses and blind, white eyeballs. They slashed at her with their long claws, thrashed at her with dead seals and walruses whose tusks made deep and bloody wounds in Kakuarshuk's side.

She ran, while she was able to run, but as more and more trolls attacked, fell to her knees and crawled, sobbing and calling for help. The trolls kicked and rolled her down endless rocky subterranean passageways, but just when she decided her life was at an end, a soft paw closed around her hand and drew her aside into a daylit shaft.

While the blind trolls blundered by, cursing and groping and kicking,

the red fox kept its paw to its lips. Then, when they were gone, it helped her upward, up the shaft of what seemed like a well.

Kakuarshuk lost consciousness as they neared the light. A terrible, irresistible desire to sleep overwhelmed her, and she was afraid that, as she fell asleep, her hand might slip out of the silky paw of her dear red fox. . . .

When she woke, she was asleep on the floor of her own hut. Around her were the smiling, familiar faces of her neighbors, making strange gurgling and cooing noises in the backs of their throats.

"They've all become babies while I was away!" she thought, with a moment's panic. Then she realized her neighbors were talking to the baby in her arms.

"I hear you found yourself a fine son, Kakuarshuk," said the *angekkok*, putting his head in at the door. "I wish you joy of him, and few tears."

Kakuarshuk thought of the other side of the world, and even in that moment of perfect happiness — *because* of that perfect happiness — she knew exactly what had made her mommy-baby cry: one day she too would have to let this tiny person go out alone into the great big world.

Isis and Osiris

AN EGYPTIAN MYTH

IN THE Ship-of-a-Million-Years, Shu rolled the dice.

"Again!" groaned Troth. "You win again!" And so the God of Mischief won from the God of Time a whole stash of minutes — enough, in fact, to make a day. And on that new day, Nut, wife of the Sun God himself, gave birth. Her peevish husband had cursed her for her childlessness all year round. But on the 366th day of the year, using borrowed time, Nut was at last able to give birth to four babies. She hid them on Earth, as kings and queens: Set and Nephthys, Isis and Osiris.

Set could find no one on Earth fit to be his wife — no one, that is, but his sister Nephthys. So he married her, and they became King and Queen of Nubia. Their love was so great for one another that they had none left for the people of Nubia.

Osiris could find no one on Earth fit to be his wife — no one, that is, but his sister Isis. So he married her, and they became King and Queen of Egypt. Their love for one another was so great that it spilled over onto their Egyptian subjects.

In those days, mortals knew nothing about clothing themselves, growing food, taking shelter from the burning sun. Up until then, they had simply grubbed about like brute beasts. But Osiris taught them how to brew beer and to dance, and Isis taught them how to weave linen, farm crops, make bricks out of the Nile mud. King and Queen were greatly loved for their teaching; greatly repaid for the love they lavished on the people of Egypt.

"What a beautiful statue!" cried Isis as she took her place at the banqueting table. Set had invited all his neighboring kings and queens to a marvelous feast and, naturally, Isis and Osiris were guests of honor.

"Aha, no statue, this!" laughed Set agreeably, and showed off his latest work of art. It looked like the figure of a man, but there were hinges on one side and latches on the other, and it opened like a trunk. The space inside was just the size and shape of a man. "If anyone here fits the space exactly, he shall have the chest as a present!" Set announced — astonishing generosity, given that the chest was inlaid with turquoise faience, gold, silver, and lapis lazuli.

Up they trooped, those well-fed kings, to try the chest for size. But either they were too fat to squeeze in, or too short to fit. Only Osiris, willowy and tall, fitted to perfection. (But then, of course, it had been tailor-made for him.)

BANG! Set slammed shut the lid and sprang the latches.

"No, no!" cried Isis. "He won't be able to breathe!"

"All well and good, then!" sniggered Set. "All my life I have had to watch you and him wallowing in the worship of your loving subjects. Now all that love will come to me — Set — ruler of Nubia *and* of Egypt!" His troops picked up the chest and ran with it, and though Isis tried to follow, Set held her fast until the coffin-bearers were out of sight.

Alone and bereft, Isis walked north from Nubia back into Egypt along the muddy gulch that called itself the Nile. As she walked, she wept —

large brilliant tears that, in falling, startled tufts of dust from the ground. Rivulets of tears became pools, pools became streams, streams swelled the trickling Nile to a river, a torrent. It overspilled its banks, swamping the countryside from the fifth cataract to the delta plain.

"Stop crying! Don't cry!" said a little voice. Other voices joined it. "Please, Queen Isis! Don't cry anymore!"

She blinked down and saw seven scorpions gazing up at her with bulging eyes, imploring her to stop. "If you cry anymore, the flood will wipe out Egypt!" they said. "We'll help you look for Osiris. Everyone will help you!"

It was true. Isis and Osiris were so loved that all Egypt was ready to join in the search for Osiris, shut up in his airless coffin, stifling to death with every passing second.

Looking over their shoulders, the troops of Set saw the Nile floods rolling down on top of them and ran for their lives. They flung aside the jeweled sarcophagus, and the floodwaters of Isis's tears caught it and swept it from swamp to reed bed, reed bed to river, from river's reach to cataract, on down the Nile.

With the help of the scorpions, Isis herself found it. Transformed by magic into a sparrow hawk, she was searching, with hawkish eyes, from high in the sunny Egyptian sky. Suddenly she glimpsed the chest floating in midriver! But her borrowed wings were weary, her bird body on the brink of exhaustion. All she could do was fly down and perch her hawk's weight on the floating coffin, pecking feebly at the lid.

Her feet felt the beat of a heart through the inlaid lid. Not dead yet, then! Half mad with hope, she pecked furiously. Her beak made a hole. The soul of Osiris struggled like a flame through that hole, and singed the feathers of the sparrow hawk!

But, powerless to free him, Isis fell exhausted from the casket and was washed up on the riverbank, while the sarcophagus floated on its way into the maze of delta rivulets, and on out to sea. There, waves washed over it, splashed in at the hole her beak had made, filled the trunk with sea brine.

When Isis awoke, bedraggled on the Nile mud, she found she was expecting a baby — Osiris's son. She was forced to call off her futile search until after the baby was born.

Not for a year, not for a handful of sorry years did Isis finish her search for the treacherous casket. It had embedded itself in the trunk of a young tamarisk tree, and the tree had grown up around it, imprisoning the sarcophagus in yet another layer of wood. Only love guided her to it, only absurd, indestructible hope made her hack her way into its sea-filled compartment.

But Osiris was long since dead.

"Dead and never to be buried!" cried a cruel voice behind her. It was Set, as dogged in his hatred as she had been in her love. He, too, had searched the Red Land and the Black for the lost casket. Bodies could be buried. Graves could become shrines. People could worship at shrines, adoring the memory of the dead; and Set was determined no one but he should be worshiped throughout the length and breadth of Egypt.

So he took an axe and, in front of his sister's horrified eyes, hacked the body of Osiris into fourteen pieces, flinging them into the Nile. "*Now* love him — what you can find of him!" jeered the murderous Set as the speed-ing river carried away the parts and pieces of Osiris.

This time Isis did not cry. She tore her hair and rent her fine linen robes, and she screamed like a gull out at sea. *"A boat!"* she shrieked at the people nearby. "I must gather up the pieces of my husband and give him decent burial! Make me a boat, for the love of pity!"

"But there are no trees to build a boat!" said the people. "No trees between here and Memphis!"

"Then cut rushes and make a boat from them!" howled Isis, filling her fists with papyrus reeds and shaking them at the sky.

"The crocodiles will tear it apart!" said the people. But they built the boat. And Isis sailed it, too, careless of whether the green Nile crocodiles, large as boats and monstrous with teeth, tore her or her craft in pieces. Blind to their green raft of bodies closing in, she sailed up and down, reaching into the water, reaching into the bloodstained reeds.

"Why do you not fear us?" demanded the largest of the crocodiles. "Why do you trespass on our river? Why do you brave our hunger?"

"What do I care about drowning or being eaten?" answered Isis. "Haven't

I pain enough already to fill three worlds? Haven't I lost my darling, body, brain and heart?" And she told the crocodiles (there were several hundred jamming the river now, like logs) the whole story of her husband's murder.

By the time she finished, the logjam of crocodiles were sobbing and tossing their green jaws from side to side in grief. Some laid water lilies in the bow of the boat, to comfort her. "Oh, beautiful lady!" wailed the largest. "We shall cruise the Nile from source to sea and find you every part and piece of Osiris!"

In their baggy green jaws they brought the pieces, as gently as they carried their own eggs. They found every piece but one (which was not important), and Isis took all her husband's remains and carried them ashore.

Far inland she walked, to a place called the Valley of Stones, all boulders and hot rocks cracking in the sun. Only then, in that desolate place, did she really feel her loss. For what good are the parts of a dead man, except for burial in the parched ground? She raised such a clamor of grief that the sky above her quaked. The Ship-of-a-Million-Years, barge of the gods, hurtled about.

"What's that row?" asked Ra, Sun and father of the gods.

"Just a mortal weeping over the body of her mate," he was told.

"Then for Heaven's sake, someone make her stop!" grumbled the ancient Maker-of-the-World. "Or how can I sleep?"

Leaning over her parcel of woe, Isis saw the black shadow of a jackal loom over her. "No! You shan't eat him!" she cried, throwing herself across the body.

"Please," said Anubis, the jackal-headed god, keeper of secrets. "Don't upset yourself. I have come to help."

The arts he showed her that day had never been seen before on Earth: how to bandage and anoint a body, how to clothe it in prayers. "Now," Anubis said, stepping back from his work, "now it is only a question of how much you love Osiris."

She called his name. She shouted out her love. She called so loudly that even in the World-under-the-World, the great serpent of Chaos heard it and flinched.

Anubis grinned a doggy grin. He reboarded the Ship-of-a-Million-Years, and it sailed on across the heavens toward the Gate of Sunset, leaving Isis and her husband in the Valley of Stones . . . hand-in-hand and talking.

He could not stay long, of course. The Living and the Raised-to-Life cannot live in the same world. Osiris left to become King of the Westerners, guardian of the spirits of the Dead. After that, when Egyptians came to die and make the long journey west out of the living world, they no longer feared the darkness of dissolution. They knew that a familiar face would be waiting to greet them in the Land of the West: Osiris, who would raise them to life with love, just as love had resurrected him.

Nor was Isis left lonely for long on the Earth. Shortly she won herself a place in the Barque of Heaven, alongside Thoth and Shu and Ra, Anubis, Nut and the rest. So now each night, as the ship sails under Earth, she is able to glimpse the glimmering towers of the Westerners and a lean, willowy figure waving, waving his greeting and his love.

The Call of the Sea

A LEGEND FROM THE CHANNEL ISLANDS

WHEN THE tide goes out in Bonuit Bay, it leaves rock pools studded with limpets and starry with sea urchins. Joseph Rolande, after a day's fishing, would often stroll along the beach smoking his pipe and watching sunset tinge the sea red. One evening he found more on the beach than peace and tranquillity. A woman lay up to her waist in one of the rock pools — as though taking a bath, but crying bitterly into hanks of her long salt-spangled hair. At the sight of her, Joseph blushed and turned away, for she was wearing not a stitch of clothing. But she called out in panic: "Please! Don't go! Help me! I stayed too long! The tide went out and left me stranded here. Carry me down to the sea or I shall die!" As she reached out toward him, he glimpsed the ripple of scales and a huge tail fin.

"Oh, no! Oh, no!" said Joseph, backing away. "You're a mermaid, and I've heard what mermaids do! I've heard how you'll lure a man down into your own world and drown him there!"

The mermaid covered her face with her hair. The water was trickling out of the pool and little by little her shining tail was being laid bare. "I'll die if I dry!" she sobbed.

Joseph was a good man. Besides, she was far too beautiful a creature for the world to lose. So lifting her in his arms — she smelled of salt and sea pinks — he carried her past the third wave, where she spilled out of his arms like a shining salmon.

"Thank you!" she cried, swimming around his thighs, her hair brushing his hands. "Come with me and let my father reward you! He's king of the sea people, and his treasures fill the sea caves."

"Oh, no! Oh, no!" said Joseph, stumbling out of the water. "I've heard how your kind lure a man to his destruction. Be off, you and your salt-sea magic!"

Something sharp pricked his palm. She had slid the amber comb from her hair and was pressing it into his hand — a gift, a thank-you present. "If you ever need my help, pass this three times through the water and I will come." With a thrash of her gleaming tail, she was gone.

Those words were like seeds in his brain that sprouted and grew, taking over his every thought. He walked the beach every evening, looking in the rock pools for stranded mermaids. Instead of forgetting her, the features of her face grew clearer in his mind. Those eyes. That mouth. That beauty. Time and again he found himself, without knowing how, down at the water's edge, searching the waves for a glimpse of mermaid. And when he slept, he dreamed mermaid. The amber comb was always in his head when he woke.

"So that's your magic, is it, woman?" thought Joseph. "That's how you mean to lure me to my death. Well, I'll not give you the satisfaction!" And he left the fishing, left his seashore cottage, and moved inland to farm a field of kale. He put a mountain between him and the sea.

And yet when the sun shone, it drew up seawater to form the rain clouds that gathered over Joseph's field of kale. It was the sea that rained on his roof.

One night, the rain beat on Joseph's roof like a thousand galloping hooves. A storm worse than anyone could remember rived the sea to a frenzy of leaping waves. It drove a ship onto the Bonuit rocks, and the Bonuit distress rockets went up.

Every soul who lived in the bay ran to the shore and peered through the downpour. Rain beat so hard on their faces they could barely lift their eyelids. Waves heaved themselves up to the height of church steeples, and fell in crashing ruins against the shore. All but one of the little boats lying along the shore was overturned and smashed. The screams of the sailors clinging to the wreckage on the rocks were all but washed away. "It's hopeless. No one can get to them," said one of the men watching.

"Help me launch my boat!" shouted a voice behind them. Joseph Rolande came running down the beach. There was grass on his boots from his run over the hill, but he was dressed once more in his fisherman's clothes. Only his boat had not been smashed.

He and his boat disappeared beyond the mountainous waves into the

hellish maelstrom of Bonuit Bay, where rocks chew each wave to shreds and wicked currents knot and braid beneath the surface. Only when the lightning flashed could those onshore glimpse the little rowing boat and the pounded wreck with its sad clutch of crew.

The lightning burst and faded; it scorched eyes, it colored the sea. But surely they could not *all* have been mistaken? There was someone else besides Joseph out there . . . a gigantic fish? A drowning woman?

"You called me with my comb and I came, Joseph. At last you called me!"

"Help me save these men!" he shouted back, his mouth full of rain.

And she did. With all the tenderness of a human woman, she caught up each sailor washed off the wreck, and swam with them to Joseph's boat. Half dead with drowning, half mad with fear, they hardly remembered afterward how they had escaped death. But many of the seventeen sailors saved that night spoke of a woman holding them in her arms, of a man pulling them aboard laughing as he did so and crying, "All this time! All this time! What a fool I was!"

To and fro he went between the wreck and the shore. As the last sailor slumped like a wet fish into the bottom of Joseph's boat, and he pulled for shore one last time, the mermaid swam alongside, her hair flowery with sea foam. "All this while I thought you had forgotten me!" she called.

"All this while I thought your kind was wicked — that I mustn't give in to your beauty! Thank you for coming. Thank you for helping!" Joseph shouted above the storm's clamor.

He beached the boat, and the locals crowded around, praising his bravery. But as they helped the rescued sailors up the beach to shelter, they looked back only to see Joseph pushing his boat once more into the dreadful surf. Had he seen another soul to rescue?

"No! You've done enough! Don't go, Joseph!" they called, but their voices were snatched away by the wind.

Joseph put out to sea and never returned. He did not need to. Someone was waiting for him beyond the third wave — "And all this time you were a true friend!" — someone with an amber comb in her hair and in her hand the keys to the Kingdom of Undersea.

Dear Dog

A JAPANESE MYTH

GOD KNOWS, the old man and his wife had little enough to call their own. There was rarely enough food on their plates, enough fuel for a fire, or enough money to repair the roof when it let in the rain. But they did have a dog and a pretty garden, too, and, in those, Sane and Sode believed themselves rich indeed.

A cherry tree grew in the garden — Sane's pride and joy. When it put on its blossoms in the spring, no princess in all Japan was more glorious. The milky foam of blossom sat like a blessing over the little garden, and every morning Sane and Sode would stand, hand-in-hand, gazing in rapture.

"Delightful!" said the old man.

"A wonder!" said the old woman.

"Woof," said the dog, and wagged his tail.

One day, the dog began to dig near the cherry tree. He scrabbled and burrowed until his paws made a hollow scratching on something buried underground.

The chest was ancient — far older than Sane or Sode or even the house where they lived. It was too heavy for the elderly couple to lift, so they opened it where it stood, and there, laid bare to the spring sunlight, were gold coins, gems and chalices, silver spoons and small vases of exquisite alabaster.

As Sane handed the treasures up to his wife, a long shrill whistle sounded beyond the fence. Their neighbor Bozo poked up his head, grinning mouth agape, eyes bulging like marbles. Nothing showed of his nagging wife but one knobbly finger poking and prodding at Bozo's head and a shrill voice demanding, "What is it? What they got? What they doing? Don't just stand there whistling! Tell me!"

"Please, please, honored neighbors," said Sode, "you must share in our good fortune. Our house is small and our needs are smaller. Please have some of this gold."

But Bozo was not satisfied with sharing his neighbors' good fortune: he *envied* it horribly. The thought of that mangy dog unearthing a mint of money made him writhe with envy. "They don't even know how to spend it!" he complained to his wife. "Now if it were me, I'd know how to make the most of a stroke of luck like that!"

And while Bozo seethed, his wife nagged like a toothache. "I told you, *we* need a dog like that. What are you going to do about it. Eh? Eh? You've got to get hold of that dog. You've got to get that dog to dig in our garden!"

So in the end, Bozo went around to his neighbors and asked to borrow their beloved dog. And because Sane and Sode never refused anything it was in their power to give, they lent their dear dog to the next-door neighbors.

Bozo shouldered a spade and hauled the dog roughly down the garden by his leash. Pointing at the ground, he snarled, "Now find treasure, pooch."

The dog sat down.

"Find treasure, I said!" raged Bozo, instantly furious. The dog whined and lay down, his paws over his nose. "*Find,* you lazy pile of flea-bitten bones!" shouted Bozo, and shook the spade.

The dog rolled on his back and tucked up his paws, as if asking to be tickled. But then, when Bozo only swore and wagged his spade, the dog finally began to dig. He scrabbled and scraped and burrowed till his paws unearthed the lid of a chest — just as he had done next door. Bozo kicked the dog aside and began to dig with his bare hands, scrabbling frenziedly for the padlock and latch.

But as the weary dog dozed, and Bozo threw handfuls of earth at his wife's feet, the chest flew open and all its treasures were laid bare. Worms and weevils, centipedes and millipedes, ants and snails, bugs and slugs burst out of the chest, swarming up Bozo's trouser legs and into his wife's shoes. In his disgust and disappointment, Bozo brought down his spade — thwack, crack — on the dog's head and killed him where he lay.

"The spade slipped. Sorry. Couldn't be helped," said Bozo as he handed back an armful of dead dog to the heartbroken owners. They wept bitter tears over their dead friend, and buried him under the cherry tree: the most beautiful spot in the garden.

The year grew older, the tree grew taller. Times grew harder for everyone in Japan. Drought reached its gnarled and twiggy hands through all the fields, blighting the rice crop, leaving fish dead in the dried-up river beds.

But the cherry tree was not stunted by the drought. On the contrary, its branches pushed outward until they were touching the very roof of Sane's dismal old shack. The boards of the walls opened, the tiles of the roof were pushed out of place, and the rain poured in.

"I shall have to cut back those long branches," Sane said.

"Oh, please don't!" said Sode. "It would be like maiming a dear friend to set a saw to our lovely cherry tree!"

But by wintertime the safety of the whole house was at risk. Like a great fist, the cherry tree was pushing off the roof, laying open the rooms below to wind and rain and snow. Regretfully, the old man took his saw

and cut off the jutting limb. "At least we shall have firewood for a week or two," he said.

"No." Sode was adamant. "We shan't burn the wood! I feel sure a little of our dear dog is in that cherry. You can make it into a grinding jar for me. That way at least we shall put it to some use, and I'll think of our dear friend every time I grind my rice."

"What rice?" asked Sane, with a wry smile. "If this famine goes on much longer, we shall be laying our own old bones down in the dust beside our dear dog. There's no rice to be had for a hundred miles. Not even for gold."

It was true. By the time Sane had carved the cherry wood into a grinding jar, Sode had only a handful of rice left in the house. Their gaunt faces looked tenderly at one another over the grinding jar. "I'm glad our dear dog did not live to suffer and starve with us," said Sode, and Sane nodded gravely.

Scrrr scrrr scrrr, the pestle ground the rice in the grinding jar. The jar filled with powdered rice — filled and spilled over, making snow-white mounds on the kitchen table. The soul of the dog had indeed fused with the soul of the cherry tree, and his love for his owners was in the very fabric of the jar, making it as magic as the dog himself had been. Not once, but every time Sode used it, the cherry-wood jar filled with food enough for five, so that Sode and Sane were able to feed the whole street.

"I want it. They owe it to us! Worms and slugs, that's all we got from that wretched mutt of theirs. They could at least lend it to us!" carped the woman next door.

"But they are sharing their food with us, my dear," said her harassed husband, sucking his chopsticks at the end of a good meal.

"Typical! They just give it away!" she raged. "If you and I had the only source of food in the whole province, just think! We'd be as powerful as the Emperor himself!" And she did not stop nagging until her husband at last agreed to go next door and steal the magic grinding jar.

A handful of rice was all it took to start the magic, so in went a handful of rice.

And suddenly the room was full of humming, the air black. Flying insects banged clumsily into their faces, crawled into their ears and clothing. Bees and wasps and hornets.

Husband and wife fled — out of the house, across the garden, into the lily pond and out again, through the river and into the woods. But in their desperate rage, they had achieved one last piece of wickedness. When old Sane and Sode poked their heads in at the open door, worried by the noise, wanting to know if they could help, they saw the blackened shape of their magic grinding jar falling to ashes in the fire grate.

Weeping, Sane swept together all the ash into a pan, and went sadly to sprinkle it on the grave of his dead dog. "If your spirit was in the vessel," he said aloud, "it returns to you now, little friend. Be happy."

The weather was cold. The drought had lasted all summer and autumn; now even the dark snow clouds refused to slake the earth's thirst. And yet surely that was snow on the boughs of the cherry tree? Surely there were snowflakes whirling in the bitter wind? Either snow or . . . *blossom?*

How could there be blossom in winter? How could the flowers bloom and the fruit be taking shape in the orchards? How could the rice plants be spiking green through the bleak bare landscape, turning the whole countryside a cheerful green? The cherry tree in the old couple's garden foamed with so much blossom that the whole town came out to see it. On their way out to the fields to reap a miraculous harvest, on their way to the shrines to thank the gods for this end to the famine, on their way to celebrate with friends and neighbors, they stopped and stared openmouthed at the cherry tree, a fountain of petals splashing the sky with pink and white.

Arion and the Dolphins

A GREEK MYTH

KING PERIANDER had music in his soul. That is to say there were pleasant, melodious strains and, deep down under that, a dark, reverberating bass. Just below his cultivated surface lay a temper like a shark. He was light and dark, soft and loud, generosity itself and utterly unforgiving. He surrounded himself with artists, poets, musicians; also soldiers, torturers, hangmen.

Most prized of all his friends was Arion the poet, the musician, the genius. Arion could, in playing the kithara, pluck the very heartstrings of his audience. And while he played, he sang — words of his own invention, spare and sonorous and sublime. No one who heard him could hold back either their tears or their smiles. Even the birds fell silent to listen; even the wild animals left off hunting to listen, ears cocked, eyes closed, entranced.

Arion was a quiet man, and would never have put himself forward. But

Periander wanted the world to know that his court contained the very best of talents. So when he heard tell of an arts festival in Sicily, he sent Arion — "No arguments now!" — to compete for its prizes. "For the honor of Corinth!" he declared, so that Arion could hardly refuse.

He entered everything . . . and won, of course; trophies and laurels, chalices and purses of gold. To his shy embarrassment, he was carried through the streets shoulder-high, while young women threw flowers at him and young men begged to study at his feet. He was taken down to the harbor and carried aboard ship: a Corinthian ship bound for its home port. "Now take great care of Arion!" the crowd told the sailors. "He has won every single prize at the festival. *Every single prize!*"

Now it would be wrong to question the honesty of Corinthian sailors, but there was a saying in those days: shake hands with them, but count your fingers afterward. When they saw the prizes they welcomed Arion aboard. But five miles out to sea, they tipped him out of his hammock and put a dagger to his throat. "Sorry, harp-plucker, but it's time for you to go swimming!"

Arion was not ashamed to beg for his life. "Take the prizes; I don't want them! Just let me live!"

"Ah, but then you might say who took them," said the Corinthian captain, in a rasping, piratical way, trying on a golden laurel wreath. "Whereas dead men tell no tales. Heave him over, lads."

"I'll sing for you! I'll scrub the decks! Anything! Only don't kill me!" His back was against the ship's rail now, their hands under his armpits.

"Sing for the fishes," said the captain, and turned his back.

"One last song!" cried Arion. "Let me offer up a song to the gods. Then maybe they'll pity my soul, if you won't pity my body!"

The captain was against the idea. But the sailors could see no harm in letting Arion play before they flung him overboard. So his beloved kithara was laid in his arms once more, and he began to sing — a wild, Corinthian lament fit to break the granite hearts of mountains.

The waves curled with pleasure at the sound. The sails, stretched taut as drum skins, throbbed with ecstasy. Fish, like a million sequins, glinted on the surface of the sea, drinking in the liquid strains of Arion's song. Seagulls perched along the yardarms, flightless with wonder.

Unfortunately, the sailors' idea of music was a rollicking sea shanty. They could beat out a jig or obey a ship's whistle, but as for Corinthian laments ... "Very nice, I'm sure, if you like that kind of thing," sneered the captain. "Now throw him over." Their hearts were as hard as the wax in their ears. They dropped Arion into the sea like an anchor, and he sank as though he were made of lead.

Down and down he went through a green silent world where no music sounds but the song of the whale. Though his mouth was open, no music came from it — only a stream of silver bubbles — minims of silence in a green auditorium.

Then something brushed the playing fingers of his hand — as gently as the strings of a kithara. And a second later, a great gray flank slammed into his rib cage and another drove between his legs. He lost consciousness thinking he was being eaten by sharks.

When he opened his eyes again, the sea was a black dazzle of sunlight and his fingers were trailing through white foam. He was astride a dolphin,

his face resting on a gray back as smooth as polished marble. In elegant lunges the dolphin leaped through the water, now swimming, now flying, scarcely even wetting Arion's face. Alongside swam a dozen more, leaping and plunging, chanting their strange, clicking, whistled language.

Ravished by the music coming from the ship, the dolphins had gathered around the hull to listen. Then, as the musician plunged to his supposed death, they had caught him and carried him — like the Sicilian crowds — shoulder-high across the lapis sea.

Venturing as far ashore as they dared, the dolphins dropped Arion in shallow water, then saluted him with crackling whistles before turning back out to sea. From a nearby port, Arion took ship for Corinth and was ashore before the Corinthian ship even crossed the harbor bar, telling his whole story to Periander.

The crew were startled to see King Periander, mighty ruler of Corinth, standing watching them disembark. "I was waiting for a friend," he told them. "Arion the poet. I thought he might have come home on your vessel."

"Who? Ooh no," said the captain. "No passengers this voyage. Arion? Sounds familiar. I recall someone of that name in Sicily. Won all the prizes at the festival. Liked the place so much, he decided to stay."

"Is that right?" said Periander mildly. "How I'll miss his singing. I shall just have to think of some other form of entertainment."

Suddenly the harbor was full of soldiers, their hands full of swords, ropes, and chains, their mouths full of curses. The sailors offered to sing in return for their lives, to row galleys, to dive for pearls. But Periander was as deaf to their entreaties as if his ears had been full of wax. They had stirred up the blackest mud from the seabed of his soul and, by the time it settled, those Corinthian pirates wished they had never been born.

Arion did not watch. His mind was on dolphins, on the poetry and music of dolphins, on the sun-spangled sea and the sweetness of life, and on washing the sea salt out of his hair.

Gull-Girl

A LEGEND FROM SIBERIA

THE DAY was so hot that the cats took off their fur, the seals their skins, and even Gregor took off his jacket. The fish gaped for air in the tepid lake, and a flock of geese and gulls floated overhead like ash over a bonfire. If it had not been for his mother's nagging, Gregor would never have bothered to go hunting on a day like this.

Idly, he watched the birds sweep in to land on the bank of the lake, watched them strip off their white feather cloaks, watched the goosemaidens and gull-girls inside wade into the water and swim. Quick as a whistle, Gregor ran and snatched up as many cloaks as his arms could carry.

"Oh, no! Thief! Give them back!" came the raucous cries from the lake. "Don't take our feathers from us, or how shall we fly?" White arms reached out to him; white hands implored him. And Gregor did give back his

71

trophies, cloak by beautiful cloak. All except one. One of the gull-girls was so beautiful, Gregor could not bear to let her go.

"You're mine," he said to the gull-girl.

"I'm promised to the Chief of the Sea Birds!" protested Gull-girl. But Gregor took her promise and broke it, for he was too much in love to care.

Gregor was not a bad man. This one unkindness was the first and last in his life. Gull-girl Chaika had no complaints after she married him, and they had two pretty children as well as a big feather bed.

Life was as sweet as a melon. But every melon has seeds and, as it happened, Gregor's mother was about as pleasant as a whole mouthful of seeds.

"Call that a pie?" she would say, when Chaika cooked. "I've thrown tastier logs on the fire!"

"Call that clean?" she would say, when Chaika tidied the house. "I've seen pigs keep their sties cleaner."

"Call that washed?" she would say, when Chaika did the laundry. "I've seen scarecrows better dressed than my son since you married him!" On and on she nagged. "You, you haven't wits enough to stuff a cushion! I knew my Gregor was stupid, but I never knew he was stupid enough to marry a dumb-cluck chicken!"

Chaika bore it until she could bear it no longer. One day, when she was alone at home with the children, she slit open the feather bed with a knife, stuck feathers to the arms and shoulders of her son and daughter, and flew away with them to the Land of Birds. Gregor heard her shrill gull-squawk of farewell as she swooped overhead, then away and away.

"Good riddance," said his mother, but Gregor stamped his boot.

"This is all your doing! So you can just sit down and sew me ten pairs of boots. When they're made, I'll search the world till I've found Chaika and the children and brought them home again!"

He was as good as his word. With nine pairs of boots in a sack over his shoulder, he set off to search the world. High summer turned to deepest winter, and one by one he wore out the boots in searching.

He had just laced on the ninth pair when he reached the mountaintop eyrie of a golden eagle. There he bowed down low in respect and said,

"Mighty King of the Birds, I married a gull-girl, but she has flown away and left me. Help me find her and my two children."

Golden Eagle was astounded at Gregor's courage. "Don't you realize I could tear out your heart with my beak, or carry you into the air in my claws and drop you from top to bottom of this mountain of mine?"

"Without Chaika and my little chickabiddy children, I don't much care if you do," said Gregor forlornly.

So the eagle took pity on him and sent him down to the seashore — a long journey from a mountaintop. "Go down to the sea and see what you can see," said Golden Eagle.

Gregor had just laced on his last pair of boots when he reached the seashore and saw an old carpenter building a canoe down by the sea.

"Can you tell me the way to Bird Land?" he asked.

"What will you pay for my answer?" replied the carpenter.

"Sir, I've nothing left in the world but one pair of boots."

"They'll do," said the giant, looking him over, and he ran his plane one last time along the curve of a newly made canoe, struck his chisel against the carvings on its prow. "This canoe will take you there," he said, sliding open the wooden bow-cover — a bark lid carved with miraculous beasts and birds, letters and numbers, signs, symbols, and mysteries.

Gregor helped him carry the canoe down to the water, climbed in, and sailed away. He had only to speak his wishes and the magic canoe sped over the water, so he asked it to take him to the Land of Birds, and who should he see when land came in sight but his own two children playing on the beach.

"Daddy! Daddy!" they cried, flinging their arms around his legs.

"Where's your mother?" asked Gregor.

"Albatross, Chief of the Sea Birds, has claimed her for his own!" said the children. "Oh, don't cross him, Daddy! He's powerful and strong!"

But Gregor spat on his fists and marched right up to Chief Albatross's tent and flattened it with a single blow. When the big white bird came fluttering out, the two of them tussled and wrestled from one day's end to the next until at last Albatross, looking as scruffy as a half-plucked chicken, flapped away into the chilly sky with a dismal mewing.

Gregor kissed his wife and felt altogether pleased with himself. But Albatross had only gone to stir up the people of Bird Land.

All of a sudden, the sky turned dark with bird-wings, the wintry sun eclipsed by flocks of sharp-beaked ravens and crows and rooks. They plucked the feathers from their own wings and threw them at Gregor like black darts. But he shielded his family with the canvas from the tent, and fought back with stones and tent pegs and pieces of driftwood.

The crows and ravens and rooks fell back — only to be replaced by flocks of kites and buzzards and hawks as densely packed as swarms of gnats. All of the eastern sky was black with them, the morning light blotted out.

"We're done for now, my foolish hero," said Chaika, and a freezing wind gave an ominous moan: *Hoowoo hoowoo!*

"Not if I have my way," panted Gregor. "Fetch me a bucket of fresh water and a mop."

As though he were about to paint the heavens a better blue, Gregor soaked the mop in the water and wagged it at the sky. The water drops fell as sparkling diamonds on to the wings and backs of the flying battalions . . .

. . . and the wind froze that water into flakes of ice!

Weighed down by their little cloaks of ice, the birds fell from the sky like stones. Stalling in flight, their wings failed them. Freezing in flight, they plummeted down and lay about in thousands, winded, on the chilly ground. They were powerless to stop Gregor or his wife or his children climbing aboard the magic canoe, and long before the bird army had shaken the ice off their wings, the canoe sailed over the horizon, homeward bound.

Exhausted, the little family reached the beach where the carpenter still stood planing boat keels. In exchange for the magic canoe, he returned Gregor's last pair of boots . . . hardly enough for the immense journey that lay ahead of them.

"Look out! They've come after us!" cried Chaika as giant wings overshadowed them. But it was only the golden eagle Gregor had visited on the mountaintop.

"Here, borrow my cloak," said the eagle, stepping out of his feathers. "I want it back, mind! Flying was never meant for the human breed."

Gratefully, Gregor pulled on the feathery pinions of the naked eagle and, tucking his family under his wings, flew as straight as an arrow, home through the sky. What a feeling that was! What a sympathy it gave him for the dipping, diving, soaring, swooping creatures he had watched so many times in the past! Gregor vowed never again to hunt wild birds, or to cage songbirds for the sake of their music.

His mother, meanwhile, having no one to nag, had found herself a husband and left Gregor's little cottage altogether. So Chaika agreed to stay, never more to put on feathers, never again to fly away. And that night, the eagle robe, lying discarded by the cottage door, flew back to its owner who was swimming luxuriously in the waters of a warm spring lake.

The Curious Honeybird

A BANTU MYTH

LEZA SAT idly juggling the magic of the world: three calabashes, perfectly round and red, picked from the Tree of Everything.

"Why three?" asked the curious Honeybird.

"How could I juggle with two?" answered Leza. "Or eight?"

Leza, Lord and Creator of the Bantu people, looked down from his plateau of sky. He did not live so very high above the people he had newly created — just high enough to see what they were doing and watch that they came to no harm. He wished them no harm. Indeed, he wished them all the good in the world — which was why he had decided to pick the three calabashes.

"Take these down to First Man and First Woman, Honeybird," he said, stringing the three scarlet globes around the bird's neck. "I need both

76

hands free to climb down. Tell them that they may open these two. Tell them I'm coming, and that I will explain how to use what's inside. Also, I'll tell them the purpose of the third . . . oh, but Honeybird!"

"Yes, master?"

"Mind you, don't go opening those calabashes!"

"Would I?" twittered the Honeybird, and flew off.

Leza began to climb down the immense spider's web that hung from the sky. Though its fabric was almost too fine to see, it was strong enough to bear his weight: so much of him was sunshine.

Meanwhile, the Honeybird wondered about the three calabashes around its neck: whether they contained any magic for birds, whether First Man and First Woman deserved such a gift, and whether they would be grateful. The gourds were very light to carry: had Leza even remembered to fill them?

That was Honeybird's excuse to peck a small hole in the first calabash.

Out spilled seeds and grain, hips and haws, bulbs and corms — all good things to plant in the newly made Earth. Honeybird cocked first one curious eye and then the other over the seed . . . and could see no harm in opening the second calabash.

Out spilled herbs and spices, gold-dust and ore, pollen and resin — all useful things for a life in a new young world. Honeybird turned each marvel over with its delicate claw . . . and saw no harm in opening the third calabash.

Out spilled termites and leeches, sickness and madness, weariness and disease, the roaring of a lion, the sharpness of a thorn; vipers and scorpions, misery, pain. And Death. Slithering away faster than thought, each evil thing wriggled into the cracked ground, into hollow trees, into rock crevices and in under the beds of First Man and First Woman.

"What have you done, you fool!" Leza's voice boomed out behind the Honeybird and ruffled all its feathers with the blast of his breath. "Could you not have waited a few short moments? My people will never forgive you for this!"

He tried with all his superhuman might to recapture the wild beasts and vile evils let loose, but they were already gone, already lurking in the earth's dark places.

With infinite care, Leza-the-Infinite explained to First Man and First Woman what to do with the seeds and bulbs and herbs, the metal and the pollen. He told them how to worship him, how to get by amid the troubles Honeybird had brought on them. Then he kissed them and climbed back up the spider's web.

But First Man and First Woman did not want to be left alone. They were so alarmed by the scrabblings under their beds, at the slitherings among their flowers, at the hoots that haunted their sleep, that they picked up their belongings and followed Leza.

"He's safe in the sky; why shouldn't we live there with him?" they reasoned. "After all, *we* are more special than any of the *other* creatures he made. We'll be safe there!" And they began to scramble up the spider's web.

The web stretched. Its intricate pattern was pulled out of shape by their weight and the weight of all their belongings. At last, with a twang as loud as a hair breaking, the web shredded and tore and fell, tumbling First Man and First Woman back to Earth in a tangle of gossamer.

Leza was appalled at their arrogance, astonished at their presumption. "Try and climb up to my home?" he cried. "Is there no end to their ambition?" And he kept himself to himself after that, confined himself to his shelf of sky-blue vapor, and did not come and go between Earth and Sky as he had done before.

The Honeybird, meantime, does what it can to make amends. Whenever it comes across Man or Woman, Son or Daughter, it darts down, uttering its piercing cry of "Follow, Follow!", leading the way to golden hoards of hidden honey, to crystalline combs of sweetness, in the hope that one day they will forgive the matter of the third calabash.

The Crystal Pool

A MELANESIAN MYTH

THE SEA was not always so big, glazing the globe blue, roaring in the ears of dry land. Believe it or not, the sea was once no more than a single secret saltwater spring where an old woman went to draw water for cooking: it made her vegetables taste good.

Often and often, her two sons, Spy and Pry, saw her go out and come back with a brimming pan. They saw the pan when it was empty, too: rimy with white dust.

"Where do you go to, Mama mine, and where do you fill your cooking pan?" asked Pry, but she would not tell him.

"Let us go with you, Mama mine, and help you carry the pan," said Spy, but she would not take him: said she knew them both for mischief.

So one day, without asking, they followed her — saw her draw back a

79

cloth, fill her pan, and put back the cloth cover.

When she had gone, they crept out. They, too, pulled back the cloth. There underneath was a small sparkling crystal pool. One stride would have straddled it. Spy cupped his hand, took a taste, and made a face. Pry tried too: "Pah!" Nothing but a brackish puddle.

Reflecting the sky, the pool blinked a blue eye. It began to bubble and gurgle, gush and rush. It fountained up between their guilty fingers.

"Oh, Spy, now what have you done?"

"Nothing! It was your idea!"

Water splashed over their feet and went on rising. It swirled around their ankles. Taking fright, they ran in different directions — each still holding a corner of the cloth, so that it tore clean through. They ran, but the water ran faster, curling and coiling into waves, heaping and humping into great glossy swells that swamped the stones, drowned the desert, hid the hills, besieged the mountains. Whole villages were swept away like bird nests. Whole herds and hoards of beasts and birds were rolled off their feet and washed free of their wings and fur.

When the old woman saw the sea coming to submerge the land under sky-high fathoms of saltwater, she snapped twigs from a magic tree, hitched her skirt past her knees, and went down to meet it. In a straight line at her feet, she planted the twigs, watering them with magic words.

On came the rolling, smashing, tumbling breakers, crashing into a spray that enveloped the old woman and hid her from sight. But as their foam fringe touched the magic fence, they drew back, sucking the sand, stirring the stones, sinking with a soughing sigh, back, back, and back.

The ocean ceased to grow. Though sea now outstretched the land, it never rose beyond those magic twigs. Even now, when the full moon tugs and rucks the seven seas to and fro, to and fro, the twigs do not wash away.

But those two torn strips of sopping cloth dangling from the hands of Spy and Pry can no more cover the ocean now than a butterfly's wings can cover a continent. Nor ever will.

The Needlework Teacher
and the Secret Baby

A EUROPEAN LEGEND

WHEN ANZIUS was Emperor of Constantinople, a certain Prince Hugh, of the royal house of Ameling, came to manhood. His father was dead; it was time for Hugh to take up his rightful position as king. But he had no sooner grown *up* than he began to grow his hair *down*. He sent for a seamstress and had dresses made. He also took up embroidery. What his family and friends thought, who knows?

Now when Hugh set his mind to a thing, he never gave up. So soon there was no finer "needlewoman" in all Europe than Prince Hugh of the long-flowing hair and longer dresses.

He had his reasons, of course. Hugh had heard tell of a princess — Princess Hilde — most beautiful, most intelligent, and most wronged of women. For her father had sworn she should never marry, and had shut her away in a tower, out of reach of ambitious men like Hugh. Nothing but rumors about her escaped that tower-palace, like bees escaping a hive.

It was not done out of cruelty. Her father, Walgund, loved his daughter. Perhaps he loved her too much to share her. Perhaps he thought his brick-built tower and brass locks could keep out Death. For in those days, Death roamed as free and common as the wolves in the great green forests.

Hugh set his heart on having the mysterious princess for his wife. So he traveled to Walgund's realm of Thessaly and, putting on his prettiest dress, presented himself at Walgund's castle with gifts of gold and embroidered linen. He said he was a refugee — a noblewoman orphaned by war, without a friend in the world.

Walgund was a chivalrous man; he could hardly turn the noblewoman away (even if she did make him uneasy, standing three spans taller than he). Besides, his wife had seen the lady's embroidery. "Oh, such artistry! You simply must teach our daughter Hilde how to sew like this!" she said.

Hugh did.

Princess Hilde took a liking to her needlework teacher that startled even her. Perhaps it was that deep, rich voice, or the strength of those big hands guiding Hilde's fingers over the canvas. Or was it the unusual *smell* of that long coarse yellow hair? Within days, they were the best of friends.

So Hugh taught Hilde his best secret of all. "I have to admit, I'm not quite what I seem . . . ," he whispered, grasping her hand and laying it against the roughness of his unshaven cheek.

The weeks that followed were blissfully happy. Hilde secretly married her needlework teacher, and they spent all day together inside the grim High Tower. Then one day Hugh said, "I must go home now and tell my ministers that I've found the perfect wife to be my queen. Then I must find some way to persuade your father to bless our marriage. Trust me: I'll be back before you even miss me!" And he cut his long hair and left a hank of it in her trembling fingers. He exchanged his dress for a shirt and trousers he had sewn himself, and slipped away from Thessaly and the High Tower.

But Hugh did not come back in days or even weeks. Though Hilde sighed sighs and wept tears and yearned with all her heart, he did not come. Even nine months later, as she secretly gave birth to a baby in the loneliness of her stone prison, there was no sign of Prince Hugh, though she never lost faith in his promise and her love never wavered.

Naturally she could not keep such a secret all by herself. She told Joan, her most loyal and trusted waiting woman, who came and went with rattles and shawls and washing, and a broad smile on her lips. When the Queen made her daily visit to the High Tower to see her daughter, Joan would smuggle the baby away and hide him, so there was no risk of the Queen hearing him cry. Together Joan and Hilde kept secret the very existence of the baby boy. "What shall you call him, lady?" asked Joan.

'His father can name him when he returns," said the Princess, for she never gave up hope that Hugh would come back and claim her for his queen.

So where was Hugh? What business of state could possibly keep him

so long from the beautiful Hilde? Nothing but war — a dire and deadly war, which spread like plague sores over the whole body of Europe. Soon even King Walgund was riding out to do battle with the enemy, and in the course of the war, found himself fighting side by side with Prince Hugh.

The war ended. Weary and scarred, but triumphant, a dozen armies turned for home. Peace settled like summer dust over the hills and shores of Thessaly. Hugh traveled home with Walgund. A thousand times he had it in his mind to say, "I love your daughter. Take me for your son-in-law." But the time never seemed quite right.

Hilde woke with a start to hear running footsteps on the stairs. "Joan! Joan, quick! Someone's coming! Take the baby and hide him!"

They passed in the doorway, Joan and the Queen. The Queen never suspected that the bundle of washing in Joan's arms was really her grandchild.

'Hilde! Hilde! get up. Get dressed. Wonderful news! Your father has sent word: he's coming home today! He has friends with him. There'll be banqueting tonight; help me prepare. Think of it, child! The war's over!"

Down the stairs hurried the old nurse, and out at the postern gate. She waded downhill into the deep grass beside the castle moat, and there she laid down the sleeping baby. "Sleep awhile longer, little darling. I'll come back for you in two chimes of the church bell."

But on the stairs, she met the Queen coming down, and the Queen had things for Joan to do. "Wash the royal bed linen and sharpen the King's razor. Mull him some ale, and strew fresh herbs on the floor of the Great Hall. Then go and tell the poultryman to kill some geese for dinner — oh, and gather May branches to decorate the castle." In fact, she kept the old nurse busy till long after midday.

The very first moment she could, Joan slipped out of the postern gate and down toward the moat. She was worried sick about the baby — big enough to crawl, to cram poisonous berries into his mouth, to grab at wasps. She parted the grass. She parted it again. She stood and listened to the flies hatching on the surface of the moat. But there was neither sight nor sound of the baby, no trail nor trace. It was as if he had never been born. In the distance, the great dark forest seemed to raise its branches in anguish and rend its green hair.

As Walgund rode through the forest, he breathed deep the familiar smells of home. He could just glimpse the tip of the tower he had built to house his beloved Hilde.

"If you ever have a daughter, Prince Hugh, take my advice and lock her in above five storys of stone and behind seventeen doors of oak. Have her taught needlework and music and solitaire. Then she can't break your heart or her own."

"She might die of boredom," said Hugh under his breath, but King Walgund did not hear: he had just glimpsed the fleeting gray streak of a running wolf, and his sword was already half out of its sheath. Walgund dug in his spurs and his horse leaped forward.

But the horse's hooves all but trampled the she-wolf's den. Five, six, seven wolf cubs, with teeth like needles and eyes as bright as mercury, rolled and wrestled and yelped in a furry heap, and there in the midst of them, a little boy baby sat snatching at their tails and rubbing his face against their fur, laughing with delight.

"By the saints! What a boy!" whispered Walgund, breathless with amazement. "What I'd give to have a grandson like that!"

Hugh's heart leaped into his throat. "How?" he wanted to shout out. *"How will you ever have any grandchild at all, unless you let Hilde marry?"*

But just as the words formed on his lips, back came the she-wolf, terrible, murderous, and Hugh did the only thing he could. He leaped out of the saddle and snatched the baby from between the wolf's very jaws.

"Look what we found in the forest, my dear!" called Walgund to his queen as he rode in under the portcullis. "A wolf child!"

Not only his wife but his daughter came out to see, and yet it was a daughter Walgund scarcely recognized. Her hair was wild and loose, her face white, her eyes swollen from crying.

"She must have missed me a great deal," thought Walgund.

"She must have thought I was never coming back," thought Hugh.

Hilde ran toward the men, arms outstretched and shrieking.

"She must have thought I was dead," thought Walgund.

"She's going to give away our secret!" thought Prince Hugh.

But Hilde ignored both men. She saw only her little boy — the one she had searched for all afternoon, the one she had thought drowned in the moat or was eaten by wild beasts. Pulling him out of Hugh's arms, she covered him with kisses, laughing and crying both at once. The Queen stared. Walgund stared. Hugh stared. But Joan just smiled.

When everything was explained to Walgund, he brooded a long time before he spoke. "A man may look to his children for obedience," he said at last, "but he'll be disappointed. A man may look to his children for surprises: they're guaranteed. A man can ask his daughter to live without love . . . but then how can she give him a splendid grandson like this? Let his name be Wolf! . . . that's if you agree, Prince Hugh."

"His name shall be Wolf," said Prince Hugh, "if mine can be 'son-in-law.' "

"Then I've gained a son and a grandson, all in one day!" exclaimed Walgund. "And there aren't two boys in all Christendom I would be more proud to come by!"

Proud Man

A NATIVE AMERICAN MYTH

WISDOM IS power, so they say, and that makes Gluskap all-powerful. For Gluskap knew everything, and magic besides. He made the world, he rid it of monsters, he fought the stone giants, and sometimes, just sometimes, he granted wishes.

One day, four men came in turn to visit him. Each wanted something, some more than others.

"Please, oh please, mighty Gluskap!" said the first unlucky soul. "All my crops have died and my well's run dry! Now my wife and children are starving and I haven't a morsel to give them! When I ask my friends for help, they call me a fool and a scrounger. Grant me a bite of bread and a jug of milk, if only for my children's mouths!"

"With friends like that, you really do need help," said Gluskap, and he gave the man a cow and a whole basket of seed-corn to replant his field.

"Oh, master of the world, I humbly beg you," said the second man, bowing low. "See how sickness has scarred my face and weakened my body? Pity my ugliness. All I long for is to be as I was born, an ordinary man, whole and healthy."

"Whole and healthy is how I made you," said Gluskap, "and so you shall be again!" And he healed the man then and there, and sent him off skipping and dancing.

"Oh, Lord Gluskap, in your great mercy!" shouted a loud and scowling man. "I am cursed with a wicked temper. I scold my wife and hit my neighbors and make my children cry. Before I do something unforgivable, I beg you, take this demon temper out of me!"

Gluskap smiled. "I always preferred the farmer to the warrior. Take off your shirt and with it your temper. I grant you your wish." So the man took off both shirt and temper, and left them in the palm of Gluskap's giant hand. The Great Spirit was still holding them when a fourth man arrived.

"Listen here," said the man. "You did a pretty poor job when you made me. But I'm a fair man. I'm going to give you a chance to make up for that. Make me taller, for a start, and more handsome. I want to be admired. I want to be the most admired man in my village! Oh, and make me live longer, too."

Gluskap smiled, but not in quite the same way as before. His fingers closed around the shirt in his hand, and his skin tasted the temper left in its weave. "Your wish is granted," he said between gritted teeth.

But the man did not thank him. In fact he didn't say a word. His feet had burrowed deep into the ground, and his spine had stretched, tall and erect. His hair had lengthened, too, so that now it was spiky and . . . green. There he stood: a fine, tall fir tree, as beautiful as any in the forest.

It is true, he did tower over mere men as they rode by; and those passing travelers did admire him immensely. And though they must have grown old and died since then, the fir tree is still there, thriving, to this day. But whether this height and elegance and admiration and long life were quite what the man had in mind, no one will ever know, because the only noise to come from him is the creak of timber and the singing of birds.

Such were Gluskap's powers. Such was his wisdom.

Perhaps you know someone like him; someone who is always right? Someone perfect who never makes a mistake? Yes. Such people can be . . . wearing, to say the least.

A day dawned when Gluskap's wife had had too much of her husband's marvelous wisdom and (it has to be said) his almighty conceit.

"Of course, there is *someone* who can resist your great powers," she said, slipping the comment in between the porridge and bread of breakfast.

"I suppose you mean yourself?" said Gluskap, all set to turn her into a sheep or a bush.

"Heavens, no! I mean him," and she pointed to the baby wriggling on the mat beside the fire.

"Oh, nonsense!" said Gluskap with a tolerant, condescending chuckle. He whistled to catch the baby's attention, and the boy looked up and smiled. "You see?"

"Hmmm," said his wife, unimpressed.

So Gluskap called the child to come. But the little baby just smiled and stayed put.

Gluskap put on his most important and solemn face, and summoned the child in ancient words of antique magic.

. . . But the baby just crawled off and played with a feather.

"COME HERE THIS INSTANT!" bawled Gluskap, and although the child's face crumpled, he only crawled to his mother and hid among her skirts. She did not say, "I told you so." She did not even smile behind her hand. No, she was wise enough simply to take the baby in her arms and sing him to sleep.

By that time, Gluskap had swallowed his pride, and come to see that there was indeed someone in the world who knew more than he — at least about babies. He took the lesson to heart.

"Wife," he said. "It's a wise man who knows his limitations."

Workshy Rabbit

A WEST AFRICAN LEGEND

THEY SAY that rabbits hate hard work, but that's a filthy slur on rabbits. I know of one who put himself to infinite pains, took tremendous trouble, expended endless energy on a project . . . even if it was to get out of working. Of course, it happened long ago — before most animals had ever met, and before they knew how each other looked. Only Rabbit, who scurried about seeing all that was to be seen and getting what was to be got, knew that here lived wildebeest and there a tortoise, here a lion and there a jackal, here an elephant and there a giraffe.

The corn needed planting, so Rabbit went to Elephant and said, "We animals should help one another. If you'll push down the trees to clear the ground, I will burn them." Elephant agreed at once, and spent all day barging trees out of the ground with his massive head. It was hard work:

91

he was not the biggest of his breed.

Meanwhile, Rabbit went to Giraffe and said, "I've done all the hard work rooting out the trees. If you burn off the timber, we can plant as soon as the rains come. We animals should cooperate, don't you agree?" Giraffe agreed. She burned off the fallen timber, amazed that little Rabbit had been able to flatten so many trees single-handedly.

The rains came in like blades of silver slicing through the heat and drenching the ashy earth of the clearing. Rabbit went to Elephant and said, "If you do the sowing, I'll do the hoeing." Which Elephant did.

Then Rabbit went to Giraffe and said, "I've done the sowing. It's your turn to do the hoeing." Which Giraffe did.

The corn grew tall and golden. When it was ripe, Rabbit went to Elephant and said, "You reap and afterward I'll gather . . . oh, but look out for an animal called Giraffe. I hear she's a terrible thief of ripe corn." Elephant slashed down the corn with scything sweeps of his long tusks, but of Giraffe he saw not a nose nor a neck.

Meanwhile, Rabbit went to Giraffe and said, "I've reaped the corn. Time for you to gather up the cobs . . . but do look out for that thieving beast called Elephant; he'd steal the corn from his own granny." Giraffe gathered up the corncobs into a pile almost as high as her head, but of Elephant

she saw not a tail nor a trunk.

Rabbit sat by and watched, just working up an appetite. "Reckon that Elephant is bound to come sniffing around tomorrow, wanting to steal our corn," he called out to Giraffe.

"He'll be sorry if he does," said Giraffe, stamping all four elegant feet in turn.

Before going to bed, Rabbit called on Elephant, too, and said, "Reckon that Giraffe may come filching our corn one day soon."

"She'll regret it if she does!" snorted Elephant.

Now the plan was that Rabbit would get up early the next day and help himself to as much corn as he wanted before the others arrived. They would simply blame each other for the theft.

But Rabbit overslept: he had quite worn himself out with all that to-ing and fro-ing and mischief-making. When he got to the field, Giraffe was already there. Rabbit thought once and thought again.

"Oh! Look out! Here comes that thieving Elephant to help himself to our corn!" he cried.

"Where? Where?" said Giraffe, baring her teeth and bridling.

"There! There!" said Rabbit, pointing to a mountain.

"Over that mountain?" said Giraffe.

"What mountain?" said Rabbit. "That IS Elephant!"

At that, Giraffe's long legs bowed and her neck sagged and her ears hung down like yellow banana peel. "God help us! We can't fight a monster like that!" she cried, and promptly fainted clean away.

Rabbit took the opportunity to nibble a breakfast of corn, tossing the chewed husks all around. Before long, around the mountain and down the road came Elephant — not the biggest of his kind — looking all around him for corn thieves. "Seen any sign of that Giraffe?" he asked Rabbit, and Rabbit nodded furiously.

"Yes! She was here just now! See where she made a start on our corn! She said it was so sweet, she'd fetch her mate, and together they would polish off the lot!"

"What nerve! Didn't you chase her away, the impudent whippersnapper?" asked Elephant, outraged.

Rabbit wiffled his nose and trembled his ears and looked as timid as any . . . well, as any rabbit. "Who me? Tackle a brute like that? Giant Giraffe?"

"Why? Is she very big?" snorted Elephant, contemptuous and swaggering. "Not too big for *me* to handle, I'll bet!"

Rabbit spread his paws wide, seeming to search for some way of describing the enormity of Giraffe. "Well, look, that's her guitar lying on the ground," he said, pointing at the the sprawling Giraffe. "That will give you some idea how big she is."

At that, Elephant folded his ears on top of his head, picked up his big feet, and took off at a run. "That's her guitar. In that case I'm getting out of here before she uses me for a bongo!"

As soon as Giraffe came around, she, too, hurried to make her exuses and leave. "Never really liked corn much, anyway," she said. "You have it, Rabbit. You eat what you can before that Elephant gets here. Look at the size of him! Big as a hill! Big as a mountain, almost! I'm off!" And away she ran, stretching out her long neck for all the world like the fretboard of the world's largest guitar.

So Rabbit had plenty of time to eat his crop of corn, all the time in the world to laze in the sun and figure out why God made Elephant so big and Giraffe so tall . . . but gave all the brains to rabbits.

Monkey Do:
The Story of Hanuman

A HINDU MYTH

FOURTEEN THOUSAND giants Prince Rama slew in a single day, and the only one left alive crawled to the feet of Ravana the Demon King, with news of the defeat.

"All my warriors dead?" raged Ravana, tossing his ten heads till they cracked together and thrashing the air with his twenty arms. "Well, if my fighting men can't kill him, at least I can break his heart! I shall rob him of that perfect wife of his!" So, mounted in his magic chariot, scorching the forest with the sparks from its wheels, Ravana snatched Sita — lovely Princess Sita — by her hair and carried her off. The sap in the flowers froze at the sight of it; the birds in the trees choked on their song. Rivers stopped flowing, and the moon flushed sickly green. "Sita! Sita! What is life without Sita?" cried the whole realm of nature.

95

Sooner than see Sita in the clutches of the vile Demon King, the King of Vultures hurled his very life under the chariot's wheels. The horses shied and smashed loose, the bladed wheels clashed together like cymbals, and the chariot sagged, buckled, and broke apart.

. . . But Ravana simply took to the air, Sita's hair still twined around one of his twenty arms, his ten ghastly mouths laughing aloud. The treetops lashed in lament, parakeets shrieking, monkeys jabbering in the topmost branches. Seeing a family of monkeys gazing at her with round, stricken eyes, Sita pulled the golden bangles off her wrist and threw them, calling, "Tell Rama! Tell Prince Rama!"

The monkeys caught the bangles in clever paws and were gone, swinging away under the leaf canopy. Beneath the winged chariot, forest gave way to shimmering sea.

Rama was picking lotus flowers when the Monkey General found him: Hanuman, Chief of Staff to the King of Monkeys and most marvelous of all his breed. "Stir yourself, my prince! Ravana the Revolting has ravished away your wife! You and I have work to do! My troops and tricks are yours to command, but we must hurry!"

"Where has he taken her?" asked Rama, jumping to his feet.

"No one knows, but my monkey millions are already searching!"

As the monkeys soon discovered, Ravana had taken Sita to the island of Sri Lanka. There, on the highest mountain, he had a palace — a mirage of loveliness built by the gods themselves, but annexed by the ugly and the wicked. Out of the jungles of the world, the monkey millions rallied to Hanuman's battle cry: an army of apes ready to lay down their lives for the lovely Sita. But between them and the Princess stretched the impassable straits of Pamban, swilling with monsters. On the seashore, the frustrated monkey cohorts bared their teeth at the unfriendly sea.

But Hanuman had magic. He wore the very wind in his tail! What is more, he could change shape whenever he chose. There, on the overcrowded beach, he began to grow, until his legs were large as siege engines, flexed like catapults, powerful enough to propel him over surf, over sea, over miles of sea! A veritable mountain of monkey. A great gasp went up from his monkey warriors as Hanuman made that prodigious leap. In a second, he was only a speck in the sky, and a hooting, whooping shout followed him out over the water. But a terrible silence followed.

Out of the ocean depths, bigger than a breaching whale, reared up the head of the Naga-Hag. Green-tressed with slimy seaweed and pocky with barnacles, her mouth gaped, dark, wet, and jagged. Powerless to stop himself, Hanuman hurtled inside.

The Naga-Hag meant to chew on Hanuman and swallow him down. But the Monkey General used his magic to grow still larger, wedging his head into the roof of her mouth, his feet into her hollow teeth. And he forced open her jaws as wide as they would go. Then, with a flick of his magic tail, Hanuman was tiny as a flea: he shot out of her ear, leaving her teeth to clash shut on her tongue. *"Ahhooeurghh!"*.

Back on the beach, Prince Rama exhorted the monkeys, "Build me a bridge! A bridge, my friends! We must reach Sri Lanka!"

They built it not from wood or canes, but from clasped hands, linked tails, and braced backs. Balancing with acrobatic skill, monkey on monkey on monkey, they bridged the Pamban.

Meanwhile, Hanuman landed — softly, softly, magic monkey — on Sri Lanka, and entered Ravana's palace. His green eyes blinked at the sheer opulence of the Demon King's lair. Everywhere, the walls were studded with gemstones, the doors inlaid with diamonds. Banners of silk rippled at every flagstaff, and Persian carpets draped every wall, while baskets of saffron stained the air gold with blowing pollen, and joss sticks gave off coils of colored smoke. But no amount of incense could mask the rank, moldering stench of Evil. And everywhere, in every alcove and dormitory, at every sentry post and turn of the stairs, squatted hideous rakshasas, whose name means "destroyers"!

"Give me your love, sublime Sita!" Ravana's bullfrog croak echoed along the cloistered walks. "Give me your love to feed on!"

Hanuman padded the silk-fringed stairs, poking his nose in at every door, until at last he found the turret where Sita was held prisoner.

As soon as Ravana had gone, Hanuman darted inside. "Jump onto my back, lady, and I will carry you out of this cesspool!"

"Oh, I can't! I couldn't," whispered Sita, her lovely cheeks hot with maidenly modesty. "No man must touch me but Rama my husband!"

"I'm not a man," Hanuman pointed out. "I'm a monkey." But Sita was adamant: even Ravana had held her only by her hair. So there was nothing for Hanuman to do but wait for the monkey army to cross the Pamban. Nothing to do? Well, while he waited, he could at least kill rakshasas.

Thousands of these vile demons served the Demon King. Some had bulbous bodies and long, trailing arms, some elephant trunks or horses' heads. Some were giants with three eyes and five legs; some looked like gorillas but for their bloodred eyes and ginger beards. They infested the palace like rats or cockroaches, and they liked nothing better than a fight. Still, Hanuman took them on single-handedly, and by jumping and weaving, dodging and ducking, narrowly kept out of their claws. Up and down stairs they chased him, along passageways, through cellars and over rooftops. Exhausted, overheated, some dropped in their tracks, wheezing and fanning themselves. "By the time the Prince arrives," Hanuman taunted, "not one of you will have breath enough to whistle!"

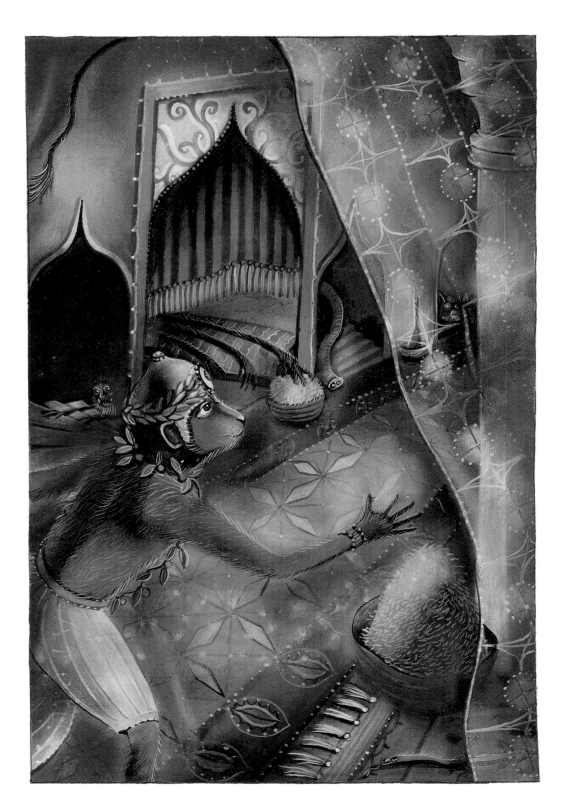

But at that moment, a lasso fell around the Monkey General's shoulders, tightened around his throat, and dragged him, sprawling and spitting, under the boot of Ravana's hideous son. "What shall I do with him, Father? What? Shall I eat him, or tear him limb from limb?"

"Monkey meat is tough," said Ravana, sneering on all his ten faces. "Set him alight and let's see him burn!"

Oily rags were tied to the monkey's tail. Sita prayed, her hands over her face, but it seemed nothing now could save Hanuman from a hideous death. Smugly the Demon King held a lighted spill to the monkey's tail; there was a smell of burning fur.

Hanuman seemed to shrivel with the heat. He *was* shriveling! He shrank down just enough to slip free of the rope binding him, and bounded clean out of the window!

From sill to parapet he sprang, from awning to flagstaff, his blazing tail held stiffly out behind. Silk banners and brocade pavilions were kindled by the burning rag. Squirming in through open shutters and with his tail for a spill, he lit bed-hangings and Persian rugs, tapestries and wicker baskets. Soon the whole palace was ablaze, and "destroyers" of every shape

and smell were jumping from the windows, or sliding down knotted sheets to escape the inferno.

That was when Rama arrived, crossing his bridge of monkeys that dismantled itself behind him into an army. A hundred thousand billion monkeys swarmed over the burning ruins of Ravana's palace, pelting rakshasas with white-hot gemstones.

Ravana was unrepentant. He thumped his chest and bellowed for reinforcements. And out of the sea came the Naga-Hag, out from the mountains came the terrible Kumbha-Karna, who could swallow a thousand men at one gulp. Soon Prince Rama was forced to retreat, bleeding from a dozen wounds. Though his courage was undimmed, his strength began to fail. He fell to his knees and his monkey legions reformed to shield him from a sleet of poisoned arrows.

"Fight on, boys!" cried Hanuman. Once more he transformed himself — into a bird, this time — and flew away. Was he turning tail? Had his burns weakened him? Was he afraid? Not Hanuman! Within the hour he returned, from the flowery slopes of the far-off Himalayas, his paws bunchy with herbs. Tenderly he tended to Rama's wounds, and before Ravana could regroup his shattered army, led his monkey millions into the attack once more.

The gods themselves looked down on that desperate day. Their hearts were stirred by the heroic deeds they saw, and Indra sent down his chariot for Rama to ride in, while Brahma leaned down out of heaven to hand the Prince a single golden arrow.

It was that arrow that finally pierced the heart of Ravana. As it did so, as the fiendish demon crashed to Earth, like a gusher of oil, the strangest smell pervaded the battlefield of Sri Lanka. Perfumed flowers of every color began to rain down out of the clouds, covering the faces of the fallen, lying in drifts upon the ruins of the gutted palace.

Princess Sita stepped into the golden chariot beside her husband, the monkey millions reformed their living bridge, and Prince Rama drove home over the straits of Pamban, his General dancing on wiry shanks behind him and squealing shrilly for joy.

Balder and the Mistletoe

A NORSE MYTH

BALDER WOKE screaming from a terrible nightmare and laid his hand against his chest. "Weep!" he cried.

His wife, waking beside him, tried to calm him. "Think, my love! What can possibly harm you? Nothing can pierce your golden skin. Nothing can bruise your soft flesh. And you've no enemies! Everyone loves you as much as I do. Shsh now. There's nothing to be afraid of." But she could not rid his eyes of terror, or the stain of that dreadful dream.

Freya, Queen of the gods, heard her son cry out. It was not the first time he had dreamed of danger, of dying, and she was worried.

"Who would want to harm our son?" snorted Odin, Balder's father and the King of all gods. "He's the darling of the world!"

But Freya, like her dream-plagued son, could not rest easy. She decided to exact a promise from every living thing never to harm her son.

She asked the birds, including the ravenous ravens, the scavenging vultures, and the soaring eagles. They all swore never to hurt Balder.

She asked the wild beasts and the tame; the savage lion, the strangling snake and all the venomous hairy spiders. They swore never to hurt Balder.

She asked the flies and the flowers, the fish and the whales, the anemones and the octopuses. And they all swore never to harm a hair of Balder's handsome head.

She asked the thornbushes and the heather, the smallest herb and the highest oak tree never to harm her beloved son. But she did not see, clinging to the oak like a lantern of luminous green, the gentle mistletoe, which grows among the oak leaves, but which is neither leaf nor seed nor berry nor twig of the tree itself.

"All is well, son. You can sleep sound tonight," she told Prince Balder.

But in the sunny woods, hidden between the tall timber and taller sunbeams, Loki the Trouble-Maker grinned to himself. A piece of mischief had occurred to him, the kind of work for which only he, Loki the Trickster, Loki the Outsider, Loki the Anarchist was designed. He saw how Freya had missed the mistletoe. She had not asked Loki for his promise, either.

Loki bore Balder no hatred, but, for Loki, a peaceful world was as loathsome as dead calm to a sailor. He needed a storm to fill his sails.

"Is it true what they say, Balder?" said Loki. "That nothing can harm you?"

"Nothing," said Balder, all his good humor restored. "Try me! Hit me! Punch me! Go on!" and he offered the flat, steely muscles of his stomach for Loki to punch.

Loki saw misgiving flash through Queen Freya's eyes; she knew how unpredictable Loki could be. But Loki only shrugged his shoulders and shook his head. "Couldn't possibly. You know me. Wouldn't harm a fly."

Even so, thanks to Loki's question, all the other gods were soon cheerfully heaving rocks and spears and trees and goats and cats and clouds and all manner of everything at the magnificent figure of Prince Balder — just to test the magic. And nothing so much as grazed his golden skin.

Even Balder's blind brother, Hodir, was easily caught up in the game.

Loki had only to slip a loaf, a fir-cone, a pigeon in between Hodir's fingers and he joined in the throwing. After that, Loki had only to slip a stem of mistletoe into Hodir's hand. . . . The tender white berries trickled to the ground between Hodir's fingers.

No kiss came with this mistletoe, no loving kindness. It flew, stuck fast, and pierced Balder's chest, sharp and deep as any needle. Balder looked down with an expression of faint surprise on his lovely face. Then he dropped like the oak tree on which the mistletoe had once grown, while the other gods gasped and cried out, and blind Hodir asked, "What? What's happened? What's wrong?"

Queen Freya held her hair in both hands and screamed a scream that shivered the glass windows of the sky. "NO!" she cried. "NO! NO! He shan't die! My son shan't die!"

Hermodir, younger brother of Balder and Hodir, ran to King Odin. "Lend me your horse, Father! If I ride fast enough, maybe I can stop him — snatch back his soul before it reaches Helheim!"

Odin did not hesitate. He tossed the reins of Sleipnir, his eight-legged horse, into the hands of his youngest son. "Tell Queen Hel she must wait for my son. Tell her we cannot spare him yet to her Kingdom of the Dead!"

And so, while the gods held their breaths, and the forests of the world quivered with shock, Hermodir spurred on Spleipnir to gallop as the beast had never galloped before.

Faster than thought, Sleipnir's eight hooves covered the miles. For a whole day Hermodir rode, and at every moment he expected to see the soul of Balder flying ahead of him toward the gates of the Underworld.

Faster than light, Sleipnir's eight hooves sped down deep valleys and ravines. For nine whole days Hermodir rode until at last he came to a golden bridge spanning a rushing river of ink-black water, and he heard, along the planks of the bridge, the footsteps of his dead brother still echoing. He knew he was entering the Kingdom of Helheim, territory of Queen Hel, Goddess of Death, but his courage never wavered. Into Helheim, into the hall of Hel herself, rode Hermodir, just as she reached out to clasp Balder's ghostly hand.

"WAIT!"

Hermodir rode between them. Sleipnir snorted and sweated and steamed, stamping his eight feet.

"Wait, Goddess of Death, and listen! The world cannot bear to part with Balder! Hodir will never forgive himself! The great god Odin's heart will break, and Queen Freya may flood the earth with her tears! Let him go! Let his soul go back to his body! Spare him just this once to his mother and father and brothers and friends! Have pity, Queen Hel!"

Hel stroked the neck of Spleipnir, so that the horse's sweat turned to ice and fell to the ground like gravel. "If all the creatures of the earth are ready to shed a tear for Balder, and if I may have all those tears to slake my thirst, you may have back your brother. I would not grant as much to any other man. Tell Freya this."

So for nine days, Hermodir rode back — across the golden bridge, up valleys and ravines, to the sunlit world, and there he returned to the forest clearing where Balder's dead body still lay, a sprig of mistletoe piercing his chest. Hermodir proclaimed the price of Balder's life.

"Then he's free!" cried Freya, laughing through her tears. "Every creature in Creation is *already* weeping for my boy!"

It was true. It was almost true. It was true of all but one. For when Freya came face-to-face with Loki, she saw no tear in his swirling eyes.

"Weep, Loki!" she commanded. "You more than anyone should be sorry! You put the mistletoe into Hodir's hand!"

But Loki would not weep. "I am framed to bring disorder where there is peace, storm where there is calm."

"Weep, Loki!" raged the Queen.

But Loki would not weep. "I was framed to trick the simple and teach the innocent not to be so trusting."

"Weep, Loki, I beg you!" pleaded the Queen, falling to her knees.

But Loki would not weep. "What's done is done, and I did it. Nor shall I shed one tear of regret. Let Hel hold what she has!" And he laughed in Freya's face, laughed and glared, dry-eyed.

"Launch a great ship," said Odin, straightening his ancient back. "A warship. Lay Balder's body on the deck. His soul will not be returning from the Underworld. Thanks to Loki, my son belongs to Queen Hel now, and is lost to us everlastingly."

But as that ship sailed out to sea — as torches were thrown into Balder's funeral barge, and its sails billowed into rags and flags of scarlet fire — Odin took hold of Loki the Trouble-Maker and lashed him in chains, buried him in the earth, and set the poison of a giant serpent to drip, drip, drip everlastingly onto the god's face.

No death came to the rescue of Loki the Unquiet, Loki the Trickster. No pity came from any creature in the wide world, except his wife, whose tears, falling in his face, diluted the poison. Now, whenever the Mischief-Maker writhes in agony under the drops of poison, the whole earth shakes and quakes with seismic horror.

Still Loki does not weep — not for Balder, and not for himself. For what he did, he was designed to do. It was in his nature to do it, just as it is in the nature of living things to die.

Culloch and the Big Pig

A CELTIC LEGEND

CULLOCH WAS cursed with the curse of Love. His wicked stepmother doomed him, out of magic spite, to love Olwen, daughter of Ysbaddaden. And the curse was no sooner spoken then Culloch fell madly in love — even though he knew neither the color of Olwen's eyes nor the features of her face. For all he knew, she might take after her giant father and stand head-high to the hills.

"Giant" is not a big enough word to describe Ysbaddaden, for he never sat in one room of his castle but he filled three — one with his head, one with his body, and one with his legs. His hair, all unkempt and uncombed, filled a fourth.

As Culloch rode up to the castle, he was greeted by Olwen herself — a comely girl, scarcely two-storys tall. Cramming her braids into her mouth in anxiety, she pleaded, "Turn back! Turn back! No one has ever asked for my hand and lived! For on the day that I marry, it is prophesied my father shall die!"

Pausing only a moment to gaze into Olwen's eyes, Culloch went straight inside. He thought, when he first entered, that Ysbaddaden was asleep. But servants came running with two enormous forked sticks with which they propped open the giant's eyelids.

"What do you want and why are you here?" Ysbaddaden asked in a slurred voice, as if his tongue were similarly heavy.

"Your blessing and the hand of your daughter, sir!"

"Didn't you know?" said Ysbaddaden. "She weds, I'm dead. It's written in the stars."

"I'm truly sorry to hear that," said Culloch. "But your life seems wearisome to you, anyway, or why do you lie on your face in the straw?"

"I only lie on my face because my hair hangs so heavy. Come back tomorrow, and you shall have my answer."

Culloch felt he could spare one day, and turned to go. But Ysbaddaden snatched up a sharpened wooden spear, and threw it at Culloch's unprotected back. Cunning Culloch spun around, snatched the spear out of the air, and threw it back the way it had come. It struck Ysbaddaden on the knee — "Ouch!" — but Culloch said nothing, simply walked out into the yard.

When he returned next day, Ysbaddaden had thought up a string of excuses. "I'm busy. I'm not well. I never see visitors on any day with a 'T' in it. Come back tomorrow." As Culloch turned to go, the giant threw another spear. This time its point was smeared thick with poison, which spattered and scorched the floor as it flew. Culloch caught the spear, spun it around one finger, and flung it back the way it had come. It stuck Ysbaddaden in the hand — "Argh!" — and his groans followed Culloch out of the castle.

Next day, Ysbaddaden, swathed in bandages, began to make more excuses. "The stars are not favorable. I never liked Wednesdays . . ." but Culloch interrupted him.

"I think we should discuss terms, before you get hurt anymore. What must I do to win your daughter? Name it!"

"Very well," said Ysbaddaden. "Fetch me the means to cut my hair."

"That's simple! I'll borrow my cousin Arthur's sword, Excalibur!" said Culloch at once.

But Ysbaddaden shook his fearful head, and set his hair tumbling through all the chambers and anterooms of his castle, lively with lice. "My hair can only be cut with the magic comb and shears of the Great Pig Troit. Fetch them, and Olwen is yours!" And he smiled at the thought of a task so plainly impossible.

"Now *that* is a quest befitting the Knights of the Round Table!" declared King Arthur, as his young cousin knelt before him in the throne room of Camelot. "We shall help you, Culloch, and you shall have your bride!"

Arthur and his knights rode with Culloch to the far coast of Wales. When the Great Pig Troit saw the brightness of their armor, saw the boar-spears in their hands, he sharpened his tusks and pawed the ground. "You may have found me," said the Boar, "but now you have to catch me!"

Twrch Troit was no ordinary boar, nor had he always been one. Once he had been a king. But his nature was so evil and his sins so many that they had pushed their way out through his skin — at first like black stubble at his chin, then as thick black bristles all over his body. His dog-teeth had grown into tusks, and his crimes had weighed him down, till he could only move on all fours: a man transmogrified into a boar. It was not hard to find him, for he left a trail behind him of crumpled trees, of houses stove in, of gored hillsides, and trampled flour mills.

Now Troit ran down the coastline of Dyfed, past Blaenplwyf and Cei-bach beach, across Ynys-Lochtyn point toward Strumble Head, then inland among the Preseli Hills. Up the watercourses of Taf and Cynin and down the valleys of Tywi, into the Black Mountain crags he ran. Past Castle Cennen they chased that Big Pig, and over the Brecon hills where Troit paused for breath.

"Hold, Troit! We mean to have those shears and comb from between your ears, but you may keep your golden crown and that ugliness you call your face!" bellowed King Arthur.

"The shears and comb are my treasure!" replied Troit in a snarl strung with saliva. "Before I part with them, I shall carve you into such shapes your own womenfolk will not recognize you!" And he charged, scattering the knights and leaving the prints of his iron hooves cut in the Beacon Mountains forever. Then he was off again, darting and dodging through the Vale of Ebbw, across Arthur's own estates of Caerleon.

Beating their spears on their shields and loosing bloodcurdling yells, the Knights of the Round Table barely paused for breath. Though their caparisons were muddy and their cloaks spiked with thorns, though their faces were masked with dust, and their horses mantled with bracken and ivy, they drove the giant boar over flat water meadows. Ahead lay the River Severn as big as the sea.

Through the shallows, from sandbar to mud bank, the boar staggered until, on the shoals called Middle Ground, he stood at bay, slashing the water to white rags. Gray waves broke against his bristly flank, and the saltwater washed it white. Arthur's knights threw off their heavy armor for fear of drowning. They whirled their long blades, wiped their spray-wet faces with their hair and, sinking up to their knees in the wet sand,

circled the Boar Troit as if he were the Round Table itself.

Afterward, no one man took the credit for snatching the golden comb. A great wave spilled Troit off his feet, and the comb tumbled through the water until Arthur's hand snatched it up.

By then, the Great Pig had gone, swimming and snorting, floating and floundering to the far side of the Severn Estuary, on and into Cornwall. Over river and hills and down steep-hedged lanes, the knights of Arthur hunted the Big Pig Troit. The golden shears clanged against his golden crown. The soft Cornish rocks turned to tin under his hooves as he clattered over them.

The knights on foot climbed up behind those on horseback. Arthur's horse was weary and slowing, but his dog Cabel was as fresh as ever, and ran snapping at the Boar's heels, vexing and harrying him with nips of its sharp teeth. In a frenzy, Troit turned and turned until his tusks were a blur of whirling white.

Spurring on his horse to one last effort, and with a sweep of Excalibur, Arthur sheared through the Boar's topknot of matted bristly hair. The golden crown went spinning one way, the shears another, and Troit bolted

baldly over the long peninsula and out into the breaking sea.

He swam on. He may be swimming yet, or rootling and ravening about the seabed, creating havoc among the fishes. But once Arthur had in his hand the comb and shears of the Great Pig Troit, he was content to let him go, out of the Realm of Albion.

Wrapping the strange gifts in white cloth, Culloch bore them back to the castle of Ysbaddaden. Culloch held his breath. Olwen shut her eyes and bit her lip. The servants came running with their forked sticks, and propped open the giant's heavy lids.

"Why have you returned with your quest unfulfilled?" Ysbaddaden demanded, peering at Culloch with bloodshot eyes.

"Our quest is complete. I bring the magic comb and shears from between the ears of the Big Pig Troit. Shall I now cut your hair, Ysbaddaden?"

Locks of the tangled, matted, grimy hair fell, with a noise like autumn. Ysbaddaden lifted his chin off the floor — it was easy now — and sadly smiled. With the merest velvety stubble around his temples and jaw, he looked quite boyish. "You are to be thanked, Culloch. Your stepmother is to be thanked for bringing you here. For what is life if it must be spent facedown in the dirt? What is a wheel if it does not turn? What is life if it does not end and give way to newness of life?"

Ysbaddaden got up, and the crowd of curious knights gathered by his moat watched him, fingers to his eyelids, leave his castle to tour his lands and estates.

"Culloch. You may consider yourself betrothed to my daughter," he said as he passed. Then he walked away, head-high with the hills, though his back was bent with age.

"Oh, Olwen!" cried Culloch.

"Oh, Culloch!" cried Olwen, and they kissed there and then on the drawbridge.

The great giant, outlined against the sky, brandished his massive club, in sheer jubilation at the beauty of the spring countryside. Then, leaning his back against a hillside, he melted way, leaving only his white outline in the chalky stone, his shape outlined in sweet green grass.

How the Fairies Became

A EUROPEAN LEGEND

BEFORE THERE was an earth to walk on or human feet to walk it, God parted Light from Dark. Pushing the darkness downward, He lived above, in the Realms of Light, beside a glass sea. The darkness settled into a bottomless tarry lake, while the upper light crystallized into spires and domes surrounded by walls of cloud. Flitting about that heavenly citadel, like starlings at dusk, were the angels, doing whatever God asked.

That was the time of perfect happiness, so peaceful that God was free to begin His next creation: Earth. Once begun, it took up all His time — parting sea from land, coloring the animals. . . . While He was away, rebellion stirred among the angels. Returning one day from creating the great fishes, God found His cherubim and seraphim brawling in the streets of Paradise. They talked of taking over from God and turning Him out of

Heaven. They had even crowned a leader to take His place: an angel calling himself Lucifer, the Carrier of Light. That was the start of the Heavenly Wars, when comets were hurled like slingshot and the skies rained meteors — God's men against Lucifer's.

Some, though, did not take sides. Whether they were cowards, or just wanted to be sure of siding with the winners, these "undecided" angels kept to the hidey-holes of Heaven, biding their time. In their smallness of spirit, they actually shrank, and their wings became transparent.

God won out, of course. Lucifer and all his troops were defeated and toppled out of Heaven. They hurtled down into the tarry pool and the bottomless region of dark. The cloud walls were mended, and everything was the same as before in the marvelous Realms of Light.

Except for the Undecided.

They scurried to sit at God's feet. They sang His praises loudly. But at once He held up a hand to silence them.

"You cannot stay," he said, and their transparent wings wilted. "You would not help me when I needed you, and he who is not with me is against me. I shall not throw you into the tarry lake, but you must go and live in this new place I have made — on Earth. Live in the hills and under the ground; live among the tree roots and long grass. From today you shall be called fairies and pixies, brownies and sprites — not angels; not ever angels."

"Do you hate us so much, then, Master?" said the tallest of the Undecided.

"I neither hate nor love you," said God, "because you neither loved nor hated me."

The Undecided who flew down that day from Paradise to Earth were as plentiful as the dragonflies and thistledown: the people who lived there caught sight of fairies every day. But somehow, there have come to be fewer over the years. Perhaps their magic wore out and they became mortal and died. Or perhaps they shrank to a size human eyes cannot see.

Some people say that God, in His Kindness, forgave them one by one, and let them go home to Heaven, and that there their magic was put to grander use, building the Universe and hanging up the stars. But we shall not find out the truth yet awhile. Not in this life.

Thunder and Smith

A CHINESE MYTH

GENERALLY, WHEN people say they don't like thunder, they mean that it scares them. Not Smith. His dislike was personal. He hated Thunder with the same seething, unreasonable loathing that a man feels for a noisy neighbor. And it was mutual. Thunder would come around from time to time and beat on Smith's roof with his ax, while Smith shouted abuse at him up the chimney, and Smith's little daughter and son sat in the corner, crying, "Please don't, Daddy! Please don't! Couldn't you make things up with him and be friends?" Their father took no notice.

One day, Smith made a cage — an iron cage too big to fit through the front door — and a long iron pitchfork. He stood the cage outside in the garden, camouflaged by leaves, then he sat himself down in a chair by the front door, fork in hand. He waited, waited, and waited for the hot weather

115

to break, watched the rain clouds fill up with dark rain, heard the distant grumbling of Thunder as he dragged his ax about the heavens. And he waited, still and patient, until Thunder's temper finally broke in the heat and he came rampaging over the countryside, splintering trees, knocking down chimney pots, swinging his ax like a hooligan.

Smith was ready for him. He put his thumbs in his ears and wriggled his fingers at Thunder, sticking out his tongue. When the god made a lunge at him, he jumped aside and, catching Thunder off-balance, bundled him into the cage with the fork.

"Aha! Eehee! Yahoo! Yippee!" Hopping around the cage, whooping and yelping with glee, Smith poked and jabbed through the bars. "Got you now, you old rogue! Tee-hee! Got you, and now I'm going to cook you and eat you, braised with dumplings!"

Thunder rattled at the bars, and chewed on the lock with his yellow zigzag teeth, but because the cage was iron, he could not break free.

Little Nuwa and her brother, cowering in the doorway, hand in hand, stared and trembled. "Oh, please, Daddy! Let him go!" begged Nuwa.

But Smith was busy saddling his horse. "I'm going to town to buy herbs — cloves and cinnamon and cardamom. I like my meat tender and tasty. You'll be quite safe: he can't get out. Just don't listen to any of his wheedling lies and you'll be fine." And away he went, down the road, at the gallop.

He was no sooner gone than Thunder trained his steely eyes on the children and began to shout at them, "Let me out!"

Nuwa covered her ears and told her little brother to go inside and lock the door.

He was no sooner gone than Thunder turned his gray eyes on Nuwa, and burst into tears. "Please, oh please, oh please, please, please!" he sobbed. "Let me out or I'll die!"

Nuwa turned to face the wall, so as not to see him, and shook her head.

"Oh please, pretty-pity-please! Have mercy!" begged Thunder. "How would you like it if a man with a cage trapped *your* father, and cooked him with herbs and spices and ate him for dinner?"

Nuwa bit her lip and put her arms over her head, trying not to listen.

"Well, all right, little one, I understand. Won't you just give me a drop to drink? Is that too much to ask?"

Nuwa thought this was the least she could do for the poor beast in the cage. She ran at once and got a cup of water. Telling Thunder to go right to the other end of the cage, she put it through the bars.

The water was gone in one slurp, and Thunder's eyes turned an interesting blue. Then, to Nuwa's horror, the whole of him began to change — to swell — to grow, bigger and bigger, until he filled the cage like a dog in a cat-basket. He bulged through the bars, bent them, burst them like a whale bursting a string bag. Pieces of metal flew in every direction, some embedding themselves in the house wall, while Thunder funneled into the sky in a single dark column of cloud. As he passed the treetops, he picked a gourd from the branches and threw it down to Nuwa, calling, *"One kindness deserves another!"*

Seeing the commotion in the distance as he rode home, Smith dug in his heels and came back at the gallop. The awful truth was all too plain: his captive gone, his hopes of dinner, too. And over his house hung Retribution: enough rain to flood not only his home, his garden, his country, but the wide world!

So Smith began work. "I'll deal with you later!" he snarled at his two terrified little children.

The wreck of his cage made the keel, and his iron barn made the walls. He was the best blacksmith for miles around and he worked fast, but long before he finished, the rain had begun to fall. First drizzle, then sprinkling rain, then a downpour, then hail and sleet and snow all mixed together tumbled out of the sky to the noise of a thousand kettledrums, as Thunder wrought his revenge.

But when Smith's iron ship was finished, the last rivet hammered home, no one but he went onboard. "What do I need with two such worthless children?" he shouted down from the quarterdeck. "Sink or swim, but don't look to me for any help: you brought this on us, and now you can pay!"

The floodwater soon came up to Nuwa's waist. It set the iron ship afloat to grate and bump about. Swiftly, Nuwa picked up a knife and cut a hole in the gourd, and she and her brother climbed inside.

The Flood rolled over the earth in swirls and eddies, joining lake to lake, river to river. Soon all the houses in the world disappeared from sight — all the trees, all the hills, all the mountains. Still, Thunder poured down rain onto the earth. People riding out the Flood in boats and bathtubs and basins called out to God to help them, but God was sound asleep, lulled by the hush-shushing of the falling rain. Their puny voices could not rouse Him.

Not until the floodwater reached Heaven itself did He stir.

Bang bang bang. "Wake up, won't you?" he heard. *Bang clang bang.* "Wake up, you old fool! What does it take to get your attention?" It was foul-tempered Smith, beating on the floor of Heaven from underneath with his iron fork, CLANG BANG CLANG.

Startled and bleary, God looked around him. He saw the earth and sky full to the brim with floodwater, and the pavings of Heaven starting to lift. "Waters, be gone!" He commanded.

And the Flood was gone.

It did not drain away, soak in, evaporate in the hot sun. No. It just went. One moment it was there, then, with a clap of God's hands, it was gone. One thousand miles deep and as wide as the world, it just disappeared, leaving a mighty long way down for those who had been floating around on its surface.

The iron ship plummeted down, like a bell falling from a cathedral steeple one thousand miles high. It landed with a single dull CLANG.

But the gourd, of course, fell as any gourd falls from trees: gently, with a spongy PLOP, into a puddle of mud. And Nuwa and her little brother climbed out unharmed.

Thunder saw to that.

"One kindness deserves another," growled the dark and distant clouds. So Nuwa and her brother planted the seeds from inside the gourd, and from those grew the first plants of the new earth, and Nuwa and her brother lived all alone beneath their shade, while the world began anew.

Cat v. Rat

A LEGEND FROM THE CONGO

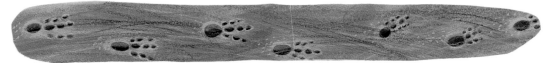

THERE WAS a time, before times changed, when Cat and Rat got along pretty well. They got on like the best of friends, because that's what they were. They lived on an island so far out to sea that the mainland was only a rim of dark along the horizon, and Cat ate the birds out of the trees and Rat ate the roots of the cassava trees.

Still, there was only one kind of bird on the island, and cassava is cassava, call it manioc or tapioca or what you will. Both Cat and Rat craved variety.

"I bet there's all kinds of food out there," said Rat, pointing with her stringy tail over the sea.

"As many different birds as there are stars," agreed Cat gloomily, "but not for us."

"We could always go there," said Rat, but Cat's fur stood on end at the thought of all that water.

"I can't swim."

"You never tried. Anyway, we could make a boat."

"My dear old furless friend," gasped Cat, "what a genius you are!"

Together they dug up a tough old cassava root and, while Cat scraped off the dirt outside, Rat gnawed out a hollow, eating the white pulpy strands as she went. "When I get to the mainland," she said, her little belly bulging, "I never want to see another cassava."

Now it so happens that cassava juice is a powerful strong drink, and by the time the canoe was finished, the two animals were singing slurred songs, trying to dance and stand on their heads and juggle crabs and so forth. They just leaped aboard and paddled excitedly out to sea.

It was much further than it looked to the mainland.

Paddling was hot, hungry work. When they stopped, the canoe stopped, too. It looked as though the journey might take days.

"We forgot to bring any food," said Rat.

"At least you ate before we set out. All that cassava," said Cat. "I'm hungry."

"Go to sleep. You won't notice, then," said Rat, and they both curled up in the circle of their tails, at either end of the boat, and tried to sleep. Cat was soon dreaming of birds, his paws making little pat-patting movements in his sleep. But Rat could not sleep. A few hours before, she had never wanted to see another cassava root. Now a little cassava sounded very appetizing. "And if I just scoop out a little more of the canoe, Cat will never know."

She scooped and nibbled, nibbled and scooped the cassava canoe hollower than before. But not enough for Cat to notice.

Next night, while Cat slept, Rat scooped and nibbled a little more. Scoop, nibble, nibble, scoop. Whoops. One scoop too many.

In spurted a fountain of seawater. The sleeping Cat felt a sudden coldness around the tail area, and woke up to find the boat awash.

"You greedy guts! You peabrain gobbling twiddler! You've chewed through the bottom of the boat! Argghh! I hate water! I ought to eat you here and now, you treacherous little scrabbler!"

"Quite right, quite right!" squealed Rat, paddling furiously while the water came up around her haunches. "I'll just help you get ashore, and then you really must eat me up from head to tail."

So Cat paddled, too, though by the time they reached the mainland shore, they were up to their necks in the briny, and their canoe was entirely swamped. "Just wait till I get my claws on you," hissed Cat, crawling up the beach. He did not know whether anger or hunger made him keenest to eat Rat.

"Oh, your lovely fur!" cried Rat. "Don't let it dry with all that salt in it! Poor dear Cat! Don't catch cold! Get dry, do! Groom yourself! I couldn't bear it if you caught pneumonia on my account."

So Cat sat and licked his salty coat till it was dry and shining, savoring the moment when he would bite off Rat's head.

But when he looked around, all that he found was a small hole dug in the beach. "Rat? Are you down there?"

"Mmmm," said Rat. "I have to admit I am."

"Then come out at once and let me eat you."

"We-e-ll. Perhaps not just yet," said Rat.

"I can wait," said Cat. "You have to come out sometime."

"I'll just prepare myself for death, then, and be out directly," said Rat.

So while Cat sat guard at the entry to the hole, Rat dug deeper and deeper — a longer and longer tunnel that broke surface under the shadow of the trees. Rat slunk off, snickering.

For three days Cat sat and waited for Rat to give herself up, before realizing that he had been duped once again. He swore then a vengeance so terrible that the palm trees shook, and rained down coconuts on his head.

So now the hunt is really on. From town to town, country to country, Cat hunts Rat, determined to kill that perfidious, cheating, no-good, scrabbling rodent. Generations of cats have taught their kittens to hate and hunt the whole ratty breed. And wherever there's a hole with a rattish sort of shape to it, you will find a cat waiting his chance to pounce.

. . .

The Flying Dutchman

A SAILOR'S LEGEND

HIS HOLD heavy with precious metals and his decks piled high with spices, Captain Vanderdecken cast off, fore and aft, and gave the order to hoist the mainsail. But the crew at the capstans did not sing as they worked. Even the surf did not whisper under the ship's prow. For the clouds that lay along the horizon were red as fire, and the wind ratched at the sea like a rasp. There was dirty weather ahead; this was no time to be setting sail.

The Dutchman was known for a hard man, but not for a fool. Though he worked his men like dogs, cursing them and keeping their rations short, he was a profiteer, and surely a businessman values his cargo if he cares nothing for his fellow men. Surely the captain prizes his ship, even if he couldn't give a damn for his crew. So, when the storm came, raging around the bottom of the world, fit to send every ship scurrying for shelter,

123

everyone expected Vanderdecken to turn back and make for shelter.

"We'll all be killed!" the First Mate warned. "The men are scared silly and there's no priest onboard to pray for our souls! Turn back, Captain, turn back, I beg you!"

The Dutchman was sitting in his easy chair on the afterdeck, smoking a pipe, while his cabin boy polished his boots. The chart lay in front of him, a single line marking a route around the Cape of Good Hope. He barely even stirred himself to answer, and then the words crawled from between snarling lips. "I'll go where I choose, and I'll kill any man who thwarts me," he said. At his feet, the cabin boy tittered in admiration of his brutal master.

The Mate withdrew, but the frightened crew went on muttering among themselves, scared of their captain, more scared of the sea that rolled down on them like a purple mountain range falling on their heads. The waves were flecked with ice, the wave tops torn ragged by the howling wind.

"If we reason with him, he'll have to see sense," said one, and led the rest — the entire crew — back down the ship to the afterdeck. "For the love of God, turn back, sir!" shouted the Mate above the racketing wind. "It's flying in the face of God to round the Cape in this weather!"

But the only answer he got was the sight of the Dutchman's drawn pistol and the sound of its hammer falling. The seaman fell back over the rail into the boiling sea — fell without a cry. But the wind screamed in the rigging, and the ship groaned from stem to stern. "I'll go around the Cape whether God wills it or no," said Vanderdecken, grinning like a fiend, his eyes gleaming. "Which of you is going to try to stop me now? None? No! Not God nor all His angels shall say me nay!"

The crew stared openmouthed, each man seeing his own death scrawled in the filthy sky. Then their pallid faces grew whiter still, as that ghostly phosphorescence called Saint Elmo's fire settled on the ship's mast like a column of cold fire.

A piece broke free and fluttered down to the deck, taking shape as it fell. Some said wings, some a gown, some a head of snowy hair, some a face of ineffable, unbearable beauty. But only the Dutchman really dared to look into the face of that blazing figure.

"Did you never hear tell, Dutchman, that it's a sin to take the Lord's name in vain?"

The Dutchman only swore vilely. "Get off my ship. I've business in hand."

"Turn back, Dutchman. Three times now you have been warned."

But the Dutchman only cursed foully and lifted his pistol a second time, saying, "Devil take you."

B A N G. The thunder was louder than the shot. And the bullet passed clean through the phantom of flame, melting into a single water drop before falling into the vast running seas.

"You have spoken your mind," said the figure. "Now I will speak mine. Every trading man looks to profit from his trade. So, from this bitter night's work, you shall earn ten thousand such bitter weeks. In return for your curse, I'll pay you in millions of curses. Sail on, would you? Then sail on forever, for your blasphemy, never touching port. No sleep, no food, no drink shall comfort you. These men shan't disobey you again, for I shall leave you no men. Hail no ships for company or aid or news; none will ever draw alongside without rack and disaster overtaking it. The world will soon learn to fear the Fleeing Dutchman, to shun him and curse him, as you have shunned and cursed me tonight!"

No tears of remorse sprang to Vanderdecken's eyes. He bit his thumb at the phantom. "Me, I thrive on terror! It's all I ever looked for in another man's face!"

"Good," replied the fiery shape. "For search the world over and you shall never find Love — no, not in one single face. Sail on, Dutchman. You have all Eternity for your voyaging!"

A wall of water as high as a cathedral burst over the ship. The Dutchman was flung against the wheel, and clung there, eyes and mouth tight shut against the swamping saltwater. When he opened his eyes again, the deck of his ship was washed bare — bare of spices, bare of sailors, bare of anchor or chains, ropes and water butts. Bare of phantasms, too. But clinging to the captain's ankle, the little cabin boy spluttered and gasped and gibbered with cold.

"Ah! Not entirely alone, then!" crowed the Dutchman, reaching down to grasp the boy's hand. But the face which turned up toward him was no longer human. It wore the snarl of a dog, and the hand he took hold of was scaly and rasp-rough, like the pelt of a dogfish. Eyes that had once fawned on Vanderdecken now looked at him with unconcealed loathing.

"My water butts gone? Then I shall drink beer!" shouted the Dutchmen defiantly into the rainy sky. "Fetch me beer, boy, and I shall drink myself blind drunk!"

But when the cabin boy brought the beer, it boiled in the tankard, making the metal too hot to hold; the foam scalded as it blew into his face. And the meat on his plate turned to molten lead. The darkness beneath his eyelids was suddenly full of horrors so terrible that Vanderdecken never again dared to close his eyes.

Without his orders, all the flags at the masthead had changed. Now, all that flew there was a ghastly yellow rag with a central black spot: the signal of a ship contaminated by plague. And though he ran that flag down a thousand times, it was always flying there again next time he looked up. So no port would grant him entry. No ship would come near.

Rumors soon spread, in cozy harbor taverns, among old sailing comrades, as they sat drinking together, sharing a supper of cheese and cold collations. The Fleeing Dutchman, the "Flying" Dutchman was a devil, his ship cursed by God. It was a ship to steer clear of, a ship damned.

Of course pirates and thieves listened in to the gossip, but heard only the words "treasure" and "gold" and "precious cargo." Far from steering clear, they went looking for the Flying Dutchman. But those that laid grappling hooks onboard, and set foot on the bare, silent decks, never disembarked again. For their own ships sank like stones, just from touching rib against rib with the ship of doom. So Vanderdecken's ship did *not* go uncrewed. Indeed, he gathered around him dozens of the scurviest villains ever to escape hanging. But they hated the captain, because they were powerless to leave him, and they cursed the day they had set eyes on that yellow plague flag, for their souls were everlastingly in thrall to the Flying Dutchman.

Restless, unresting, the ship sails on around and around the watery globe. Though the boards have been chafed through by the salt-sharp sea, and her ribs laid bare, still she does not sink. Though the sails have been blown to the ragged thinness of rotten silk, still she speeds before the remorseless trade winds. The chart on the Captain's desk is blacker now than a spider's web with the courses he has plotted on his never-ending voyage.

Endless hail and wind and sun have beaten down on the Dutchman's head, so that his brown face is scored with creases, his misery etched for anyone to see. Whole centuries have passed since Vanderdecken learned repentance, learned to crave a kind face, a smile, a hand extended in friendship. But he sees only resentment, loathing, hate, contempt, terror.

Now, the sailors in the portside taverns whisper that God's anger is softening — that once every seven years or so, Vanderdecken is seen ashore, walking the streets of some foreign port, lifting his cap to the ladies, in the hope that one will stop and listen to his story, pity him — love him.

But looking into those half-crazed eyes, seeing all that horror, hearing his crimes, what woman could ever love the Flying Dutchman? So perhaps God's anger is not lessening. Perhaps God has merely found a new way to torment His damned Dutchman from everlasting to everlasting.

The Sky-Blue Storybox

A LEGEND FROM GHANA

BY NOW, you have heard many stories. Forget them. Imagine you have never heard any; that there are no stories to hear. That is what the world was like when Anansi was young — when all the stories were kept in a strongbox, up in Heaven.

Everyone needs stories, not least Anansi the Spider Man. He wanted them for himself and for his family. He wanted the power that stories bring, the respect that comes to the storyteller, the taste of those stories in his mouth. So he wove a web and climbed up it to Heaven, and he said to Sky-God, "Tell me the price of the Sky-Blue Storybox."

"Aho," said Sky-God. "Many have wanted to buy my Storybox: kings and sorcerors and millionaires. But none could muster the price."

"What is the price?" asked Anansi.

"All the spots on the leopard, a handful of hornets, a rainbow python and a fairy. Bring me all these and the stories are yours."

Anansi bowed. "I'll be back," he said.

The leopard part was easy.

All he had to do was dig a pit and brew a keg of beer. Then, inviting Leopard home for a drink, he took sips, while Leopard drank deep. By the time Leopard reeled home he was in no fit state to see the pit in his path. In he fell, and with such a thud that his spots all fell off. Then Anansi brought a ladder and, with tender concern, helped Leopard out.

Later, all that remained was to gather up the spots . . . which left the hornets, the python, and the fairy.

At this point, Anansi felt a little uneasy, for he had no idea how to catch a handful of hornets.

"What you need," said his wife, "is a gourd, a leaf from a banana tree, and a cup of water."

"I see what you mean!" said Anansi. The gourd he cut a hole in; the leaf he put on his head. The cup of water he threw in the air.

"Hornets! Oh, hornets!" called Anansi. "What will become of you, now that the rains have come?"

A passing swarm of hornets looked at Anansi. The rains surely had come. Why else would anyone be standing with a dripping banana leaf on his head?

"Shelter in this gourd, friends, and be quick about it!" urged Anansi. "Or the rains will smash your silver wings!"

At once the hornets flew into the gourd, thanking Anansi as they did so. As soon as they were inside, Anansi plugged the hole. There it was. A hand-grenade of hornets . . . which left only the python and the fairy.

At this point Anansi was in a bit of a quandary, for he had no idea how to catch a rainbow python.

"What you need is a tree trunk and a length of twine," said his wife.

"I see that, plain as day!" said Anansi. Immediately, he went and cut down a tall palm tree and stripped it bare. Then, with the tree tucked under two or three arms, he walked through the jungle, talking to it as he went. "He is, I tell you," said Anansi to the tree, and then, "I tell you he *is!* I'll prove it to you!" And then, "Don't argue!"

The rainbow python was puzzled (as anyone would be) to see Anansi talking to a tree. "Ho there, Anansi! What gives, man?"

"My friend here" (said Anansi to the python) "says that he's longer than you, but I say you're longer. Won't you settle the argument, once and for all?"

"Of course, of course," said the python, flattered, and lay down alongside the palm tree. Around once, around twice, around three times, Anansi bound the twine, until he reached the python's head. "I believe," he said, "that now you're mine for the giving . . . which leaves only the fairy."

Now Anansi had not the remotest idea how to catch a fairy. His wife said, "What you need is a wooden dolly and some sap from the gum tree."

"Of course," said Anansi, and then, "why's that?"

"To make a gum baby, of course!" said his wife.

"Of course! Of course!" said Anansi. "A gum . . . what was that?"

"And some banana mash for it to hold," said his patient wife.

At last Anansi saw what she was driving at, and went to make a little wood carving of a child. This he covered in gum, and into one wooden hand he tied a bowl of banana mash. On the face he painted a smile. Then he propped the whole thing against a tree, and hid in the branches.

Before long a fairy came by and, seeing the figure holding out a bowl of banana mash, politely asked if she might have some.

Dolly didn't say "Yes", didn't say "No"; it just smiled. So the fairy helped herself. She even said, "Thank you."

Dolly didn't say "Stay", didn't say "Go"; it just smiled.

"What's your name?" asked the fairy.

Dolly didn't say "Jess", didn't say "Mo"; it just smiled.

"Are you deaf?" asked the fairy.

Dolly didn't say "Guess", didn't say "So"; it just smiled. At which the fairy started to feel seriously put out, and gave the dolly a push on the shoulder. "Speak, can't you?"

Dolly didn't speak fast, didn't speak slow; it just smiled. But it didn't let go of the fairy's hand, either, seeing as its shoulder was sticky as flypaper.

"Don't just stand there grinning!" snapped the fairy. "Give me back my hand!" And she slapped the other shoulder. There she stuck, like a wasp in jam. She gave the dolly a kick with both feet, and butted it, too.

Dolly didn't say "Cease", didn't say "Ow!"; it just smiled its sticky smile, hard up against the fairy's face.

That was when Anansi climbed down out of the tree, picked up the dolly and the fairy (stuck as fast together as the two sides of a sandwich), and carried her up to Sky-God, along with the rainbow python, the gourd full of hornets, and the purse full of leopard spots.

Sky-God looked at the great squeaking, buzzing bundles laid down at

his feet and his eyes were round as full moons. "What's this you've brought me, Spider Man Anansi?"

"The price of the Sky-Blue Storybox, master," said Anansi. "The gourd is full of hornets, so be careful how you take off the lid."

"Many have asked to buy the Storybox," said Sky-God "but only Spider Man Anansi has managed to pay the price, tricky devil that he is." So saying, Sky-God laid one finger on each bundle: "I have touched them; they are mine!" he said, trying to unstick his finger from the gummy fairy. "The Storybox is yours, Mister Anansi!"

So Anansi climbed down his web out of the sky, the box tucked under four of his arms. And halfway down he cracked it open and began spilling out the stories: riddles and fables, parables and sagas, ballads and myths and legends.

"Wey, Spider Man!" called Sky-God. "What you doing, man? Ain't you gonna sell them or keep them for a treasure all to yourself?"

"I know what I'm doing," said Anansi. "They're mine, so they're mine to let go!"

Pretty soon, Sky-God let go the rainbow python and the leopard spots, too, the angry hornets and the fairy; they were his, so they were his to let go. Naturally, they were livid with Anansi, and went looking for him, to pay him back.

But by then, the people of Earth were so grateful to Anansi for the stories he had spilled that they hid and harbored their hero safe and sound.

It took a while for those stories to spread worldwide, but not so long as you might think, given the size of the world. Wherever a traveler made tracks he carried a wealth of stories, to pay for his supper or a bed for the night. And that's how stories spread far and farther than far.

But answer this riddle. If there were no stories before Spider Man Anansi fetched down his prize, where did I find the story of Anansi and the Sky-Blue Storybox?

About the Stories

All these stories have been passed down from generation to generation by word of mouth and changed a little by each successive storyteller, growing and altering to suit the listener. I have retold them — sometimes from the briefest passing reference in dusty old volumes — to please you, the reader.

In doing so, I have made sometimes small, sometimes large changes, but have tried to preserve an inkling of the pleasure each story gave to its original audience.

G. McC.

Four Worlds and a Broken Stone

The Black Mesa stands at Four Corners, Arizona, and is crucial to the religion of the ancient indigenous Hopi tribe. The word "Hopi" itself means "Peace." The Hopi currently consider that the time of the Great Purification has begun, which will result in the destruction of the Fourth World and establishment of the Fifth.

Lamia

Legends of lamias are amazingly widespread. From Greece to China people have believed in snake-women deadly to their human mates, unmasked only by goodness or wisdom. John Keats wrote a poem about one. This legend, though, comes from Kashmir.

A Question of Arithmagic

Olaf Tryggvason ruled Norway from A.D. 995 - 1000. A series of stories recount his various confrontations with heathen gods and malevolent trolls, all of which give the impression that the Old Magic is more potent than the new (Christianity), though the King does always win *in the end.*

The Gods Down Tools

Creator gods are not generally pictured as manual laborers, but the Sumerian gods of Babylonia are credited with creating mankind to take their place after the gods downed pickax and shovel themselves, and went on strike.

A Bouquet of Flowers

The aboriginal peoples of Australia tell various stories of Baiame, the Father Spirit, who lived on Earth as a man for a short time so as to rest after completing Tya (the world). He promised to return to visit them, now and then, in human form.

About the Stories

THE PIED PIPER

The German Pied Piper dates from 1298, when Hamelin's children were reputedly lured away by a magician and never seen again. The legend has been used to explain where isolated Germanic-speaking groups came from — the lost children of Hamelin reemerging elsewhere from underground. Another theory is that the story masks the real-life tragedy of the Children's Crusade when whole populations of children did willingly leave their homes, incited by the Pope to fight a holy war. They never returned.

A PRICKLY SITUATION

In the orginal Haida myth, both Beaver and Porcupine are spirit animals (though Porcupine's spines are no less substantial for that). The Haida are a Native North American people living both on the British Columbian mainland and the sprinkling of islands offshore, the Queen Charlotte Islands. And North American porcupines *can* climb trees!

RACE TO THE TOP

The creation myths of the Maori people of New Zealand are epic and complex. Tane, both the god of forests and of light, is often found in conflict with his scheming brother. This battle is the third and last war to involve the seventy immortal offspring of Rangi and Papa (Earth and Sky). The original story, in fact, accounts for many very specific rituals of worship among priests and worshipers.

THE ALCHEMIST

Two thousand years ago, alchemy — the magical chemistry of transmuting valueless substances into precious ones — intensely interested the Taoist priests of China. Whereas alchemists in Europe were usually seen as in league with the Devil, the Chinese ones were virtuous Immortals revisiting Earth.

MOMMY'S BABY

This story is told by the Eskimos of West Greenland. Though only a guess, it seems fairly plain that Kakuarshuk's subterranean journey is a mystical depiction of labor and childbirth itself.

ISIS AND OSIRIS

Even after the wondrous Old, Middle, and New Kingdoms had declined, and the Romans subjugated Egypt, Isis and Osiris were still being worshiped far and wide. Her tears swelling the Nile was the mythological explanation of a yearly event, when the river, swollen by rains upriver, overspilled its banks. Though dangerous and unpredictable, it spread the banks with fertile black silt: a greater blessing to Egypt than all its gold and silver.

THE CRYSTAL POOL

THE CALL OF THE SEA

Generally, the mythical mermaid is brought ashore as an unwilling wife and ultimately returns to the sea. This legend from the Island of Jersey in the English Channel is different. It also involves historical events.

DEAR DOG

The Japanese tell countless variations of this story, the good *kami* of an animal or person passing into other living things, bringing help to the deserving, punishment to the wicked. Plants in particular are seen as selflessly devoted to those who treat them tenderly, and it is a heinous crime indeed to cut down a beautiful tree.

ARION AND THE DOLPHINS

Arion really was a poet at the court of the tyrant Periander — probably around 625 B.C., though the legend of his rescue is pure poetic licence. In an older Greek myth, Dionysius, god of agriculture, is captured by pirates who leap overboard in terror when they realize who he is. He transforms them into the world's first dolphins.

GULL-GIRL

This Chukchi myth from the bleak landscapes of Siberia is very like the European mermaid myths in which a fisherman takes a "sulkie's" tailskin and hides it so that she cannot return to the sea. Torn between husband and natural instincts, the mermaid inevitably finds the tail and swims away, mourning the children she is forced to leave behind on dry land.

THE CURIOUS HONEYBIRD

This Bantu version of Pandora's Box also incorporates the belief of one section of Bantu — the Kaonde — surrounding Leza's withdrawal from his creation. This apparent aloofness of the creator, taking offense after a period of initial tenderness, recurs time and time again throughout Africa.

THE CRYSTAL POOL

The people of Melanesia, like so many other places, widely recall a Great Flood turned back by a serpent during the dawn of time. This particular story, however, from the Bainang peoples of New Britain, accounts for the origins of the oceans.

About the Stories

The Needlework Teacher and the Secret Baby

The Langobardic cycle of legends are just as complex as the more famous tales of King Arthur. Set down in the fifteenth-century Book of Heroes, these stories — of Constantine and the Amelings, of Ice Queens, bear-witches and more — date back six centuries earlier than that. All trace is lost of whatever true-life events and people gave rise to them, but they originated in a region known then as Pannonia (now Hungary and its surrounding territories). The action roams, though, as far afield as Sweden, Greece, Heligoland, Constantinople, and Germany, depicting a war-torn Europe rich in chivalry.

Proud Man

The Algonquin tribes who inhabit the northern forests of the United States have a richly complex culture. They tell a great, widely renowned poetic cycle of stories about Gluskap (or Glooskap), their creator god, and his brother Malsum the Wolf, the evil antithesis of Gluskap's goodness. When Malsum has been defeated, the world perfected, and Gluskap's many adventures are complete, he sails towards sunrise in his canoe, watched by the animals who love him, perhaps to return one day.

Workshy Rabbit

The Hausa tribes of West Africa tell this particular fable of small outsmarting big. Wherever Rascal Rabbit pops up (as far afield as North America, Japan, and Asia), his trickery and cunning are always admirable rather than reprehensible. Rabbit rarely meets with retribution.

Monkey Do: The Story of Hanuman

Hanuman, son of the Hindu wind god, is a divine being. For helping Rama, he is rewarded with eternal youth. The exploits of the two are set down in the seven-volume *Ramayana*, one of the great epic works of Sanskrit literature, composed by the poet Valmiki in 500 B.C. Even to read the *Ramayana* is an act so holy as to absolve the reader of sin. When Hanuman's fame spread to China, he became hugely popular there, too, and the subject of new adventures.

Balder and the Mistletoe

Among the Scandinavian gods of Asgard, Balder was god of light. More than one myth accounts for his death — in one, Hodir is his rival in love and kills him in a fight — but one idea remains constant: Balder's death begins the Twilight of the Gods, the destruction of the halls of Asgard — Ragnarok, the Day of Doom. From the ruins of the Old World is born a new one in which Balder returns.